World's Most
Eligible Bachelors

Maggie Shayne

That Mysterious Texas Brand Man

D0033038

Silhouette® Books

Published by Silhouette Books
America's Publisher of Contemporary Romance

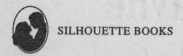

SILHOUETTE BOOKS

ISBN 0-373-65021-3

THAT MYSTERIOUS TEXAS BRAND MAN

MVFOL

*Everything you ever wanted to know
—and more—
about*

WORLD'S MOST ELIGIBLE BACHELOR

Marcus Brand

Occupation: "They call me The Guardian—protector of all that is good in this world."

Secret Yearning: "To find my family, which was taken from me years ago."

True Identity: "Not even I know for sure. But I get the feeling that the answer lies deep in the heart of Texas, at the Brand family ranch."

Home: "I live in an isolated mansion, opulent but lonely. Perfect place for a brooding and mysterious bachelor like myself, though I long for the clear open spaces of Texas."

Marriage Vow: "Some men just weren't made for vows of love. Or maybe I just haven't met the right woman yet."

Dear Reader,

Thanks for returning for another WORLD'S MOST ELIGIBLE BACHELORS book, a brand-new twelve-book series all about men—and romance! Each of these delectable heroes has been named a World's Most Eligible Bachelor by *Prominence Magazine*—a fictitious publication we editors created just for you!

We hope you'll enjoy these compelling stories written by some of your most beloved authors. Every book focuses on a fabulous male and gives you the most intimate details of the romance that leads him down the aisle to Marriageville.

Bestselling author Maggie Shayne brings us this month's delectable hero, Marcus Brand. He's known to the world as The Guardian—a mysterious man who's vowed to protect the innocent. So he just can't say no when a beauty in need requests his help...and his love. This memorable story is also part of Maggie Shayne's popular THE TEXAS BRAND series, so don't miss it!

Next month's bachelor is from beloved author Jackie Merritt. Playboy Symon Cope is about to learn how to settle down, thanks to a feisty female's charming ways. Be sure to see how the *Big Sky Billionaire* is tamed in this supersexy tale.

Until then, here's to romance wishes and bachelor kisses!

The Editors

Please address questions and book requests to:
Silhouette Reader Service
U.S.: 3010 Walden Ave., P.O. Box 1325, Buffalo, NY 14269
Canadian: P.O. Box 609, Fort Erie, Ont. L2A 5X3

A Conversation with...
Award-winning author
MAGGIE SHAYNE

What hero have you created for WORLD'S MOST ELIGIBLE BACHELORS, and how has he earned the coveted title?

MS: For my hero, the title wasn't so coveted. Marcus has built his entire life around anonymity. By day he's a reclusive millionaire, but by night he's The Guardian, a mysterious protector of the innocent, a frightening threat to the guilty.

This original title is part of THE TEXAS BRAND, a Silhouette Intimate Moments miniseries. What about this series so appeals to you? Do you have spinoffs planned?

MS: There have been four titles in THE TEXAS BRAND series to date: *The Littlest Cowboy, The Baddest Virgin in Texas, Badlands Bad Boy* and *The Husband She Couldn't Remember*. I'm planning at least three more books in the series for 1999, *The Baddest Bride in Texas* in February.

What modern-day personality best epitomizes a WORLD'S MOST ELIGIBLE BACHELOR?

MS: The correct answer is, "The one who makes his lady feel like The World's Most Beloved Woman."

The honest one—actor Adrian Paul.

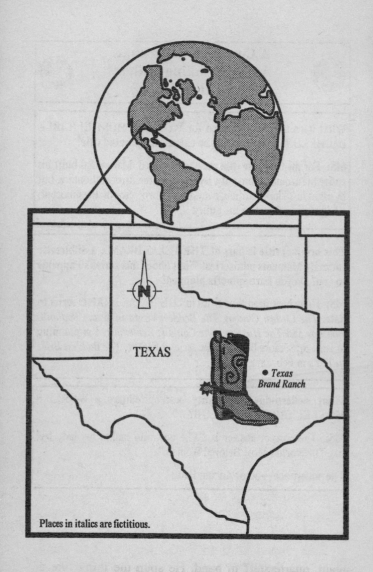

TEXAS

● *Texas Brand Ranch*

Places in italics are fictitious.

Prologue

Silver City, New York
1985

The broadsword missed his neck by mere inches, flashing by so close Marcus actually felt it.

Caine smiled. His face craggy, rugged. Fifty-two, and the lines in his face showing every day of it. But he moved like a twenty-year-old, and his cobalt blue eyes sparkled with the mischievous charm of a schoolboy.

He lunged forward, thrusting the sword upward, but Marcus dodged the blade and brought his own down atop it. When Caine's weapon clattered to the floor, the older man smiled. "First time you've disarmed me, boy. Either I'm getting older or you're getting better." He tugged at the front of his sweat-damp, sleeveless T-shirt.

Marcus didn't relax. The old man was full of tricks. He resisted the urge to swipe away a trickle running down the center of his own bare chest and stayed focused.

Caine turned as if to walk away, only to whirl again, quarterstaff in hand. He spun the thing like a windmill, passing it from one hand to the other as he came closer.

Marcus tossed the broadsword down and picked up a staff of his own from the racks of weapons lining the gym walls. For a time they circled each other, and then they sprang, and the echoes of wood crashing against wood filled the room to deafening levels.

Caine's staff broke Marcus's in two. Marcus gave a mocking bow. "One for one," he said. "Care for some hand-to-hand combat?"

"Not this time." Caine pulled a gun, a small black revolver, and pointed it at Marcus.

Marcus froze. He froze just the way he had nine years ago. And for an instant, he could hear it all again. The rapid pattering fire of the automatic. His mother's anguished scream.

She'd screamed a name. A name he couldn't remember, like so many other things about his childhood. But he remembered that day. Just before Christmas. His little sister, Sara, all excited because they were going to their cousins' ranch in Texas as they did almost every Christmas. His little sister, Sara. And his mother and his father. Dead. All of them.

Marcus hated Christmas.

The sounds faded, and eventually the smell of gunpowder did, as well. Not real. Memories. Faded, half-formed, but part of his past. Marcus lifted his chin.

"I don't train with guns. You know that."

"And I understand it, Marcus. Better than you know. In nine years, I've never pushed the issue."

"So why are you pointing that filthy thing at me now?"

Caine shrugged, lifting one eyebrow and cocking his head as he did. "You're nineteen, Marcus, and you can call yourself an expert in just about any form of combat I can think of. All except one."

"And that's good enough. I'll never use a gun. Hell, I'll probably never use any of this stuff you're always teaching me. Sometimes I wonder why you bother—"

"I have my reasons. Besides, knowledge is power."

"You've certainly seen to it I'm powerful, then." Caine had taught him everything. Marcus was fluent in seven languages, could do complex calculations in his head, knew the names of the leading lawmakers of every country in the world and could draw maps of most of those countries. He had never known why he had to know all these things. It had never occurred to him to ask until very recently. It always just...was.

"But I'll never use a gun," he finally said.

"Don't use one, then. But learn to defend yourself against those who do." Both brows rose this time, accompanied by a slight nod as if to say, "Make sense?"

"All right. What do I do?"

"Use your feet. It's unexpected, fast and effective. However, accuracy is vital. You miss, you don't get another chance. Spinning back kick or a simple crescent. Just hit the target. Ready?"

Marcus nodded. Caine lowered the gun, then quickly lifted it again. Marcus spun, kicked and missed by six inches.

"Bang. You're dead. Try again."

Sighing, Marcus complied. He'd always complied with Caine's wishes. Devoured Caine's instructions. Caine was all he had. All he'd had since that Christmas nine years ago, when the older man had come upon a ten-year-old boy wandering the dark streets in shock. Unable to speak, barely able to remember his own name. Marcus didn't know what would have happened to him without Caine. He supposed if he could love anyone, he'd love the old man. But since he couldn't, didn't even want to, he simply called it fondness. Caring.

On the tenth try, Marcus hit the gun and sent it sailing from Caine's hand. The man smiled and slapped Marcus's back, the closest thing to physical affection he'd ever demonstrated. He's a loner, Marcus thought. Like me. Two of a kind.

"Good boy."

There was a tap at the double doors. They opened, and Graham stepped in. Impeccable black suit, black shirt underneath. Nehru collar, no tie. Unlike Caine's, Graham's face was ageless. He could be Caine's age or twenty years older. It was impossible to tell. Silver hair, contrasting with dark brows. Lean, but still muscular. Fit. Marcus had never been exactly sure what Graham did besides provide sarcasm and take care of the two of them. He'd seen the older man working in the room downstairs with all the computer equipment once or twice, but he wasn't supposed to go down there, so he'd never asked. On the surface, Graham acted like a butler, but that was some kind of scam. He was no gentleman's gentleman.

"The morning paper, Caine," Graham said, very

butlerlike but with a twinkle of mirth in his eyes. As if it were some inside joke.

"Couldn't it wait until breakfast? We're starved."

"Oh," Graham said, and sniffed. "I hope there's ample time for a shower first."

Caine looked at Marcus. "I think he just said we stink."

"We do," Marcus said, and took the paper from Graham, curious. He read the front-page headline, shook his head, rolled his eyes. "It's that urban-legend garbage they keep playing up. 'The Guardian Strikes Again.' God, what a crock."

"Utter nonsense," Graham said.

"Absolutely," Caine added. "Read it to us, Marcus." He slung a towel around his neck and led the way out of the gym, heading for the showers. Graham followed.

Marcus brought up the rear, reading aloud as he walked.

"Silver City Liquor Emporium was the scene of an attempted robbery last night. Witnesses claim two men wearing ski masks and wielding shotguns burst in demanding cash. The attempt was foiled by a man dressed all in black, wearing a long dark coat and a wide-brimmed fedora pulled low to shadow his face. This man—who matches other crime-scene descriptions of Silver City's legendary Guardian—quickly disarmed the suspects with no more than his bare hands. 'He just flew into action,' Tim Gaines, the cashier on duty, said. 'And the next thing we knew, the two creeps were on the floor whimpering and the big guy stood there ejecting the shells from their guns.'

Police arrived to find the suspects bound, gagged and disarmed. The unnamed hero simply vanished into the night. 'It was him,' Gaines told reporters. 'It was the Guardian, I know it was. I just wish there were some way I could thank him.'

So if you're out there reading this, Guardian, Tim Gaines sends his thanks. And so do all the citizens of Silver City.''

Marcus folded the paper and handed it to Graham. They stood in the dressing room where the showers were now. Caine was already cranking on the water and stepping into a shower stall out of sight.

"Sensationalism, pure and simple. That and a few scared, confused witnesses." Marcus reached into another stall to turn on the water.

"You're quite right, I'm sure," Graham said. Then he turned to go, clearing his throat as he did so.

Marcus popped his head out of the shower stall to look after him. For a second there, he thought Graham's overblown throat clearing had been disguising a laugh.

Nah.

Marcus had been wanting to go out into the world by himself for a while now. It wasn't that he wanted anything to do with people. He didn't. He liked things just the way they were. It was safe behind the gilded gates of Caine's estate. He didn't have to deal with anyone—no complicated relationship skills to master. Just the lessons.

But he was curious. He didn't want to take part, he just wanted to…observe.

Of course, Caine forbade this, though Marcus never knew why. Not that it mattered. He'd always been fairly strong willed, and though he'd never disobeyed Caine before, he did this time.

He slipped out, after dark.

It was winter in Silver City. Christmas season in full swing. Snow danced through the night sky and dusted the sidewalks and cars. And Marcus walked, trying to ignore it. It was tough, though. Carols blasted from speakers attached to every lamppost. The shop windows were lined with colored bulbs and pine trees were decorated so heavily their boughs drooped under the weight. People ran past him with red and green foil shopping bags and gaily wrapped packages.

He hated Christmas.

He hadn't always. The nightmare had happened just before Christmas though, and he'd never enjoy the holiday again. Besides, he could barely remember the Christmases before that tragic one. Just vague bits and pieces. Some cousins. That ranch in Texas. Riding horses. Something about a porch swing his little sister would never leave alone.

He gave his head a shake and continued walking. He wasn't a part of this, he realized. He was different. Like some alien walking among earthlings. He didn't belong. He was no more like the people around him than he was like the snow-dusted sidewalk under his feet. He didn't interact. Didn't connect or communicate. He just observed. Detached, but interested in spite of himself.

This became his ritual, his secret, his…hobby, if you wanted to call it that. This observing.

Until one night, when he came upon something he couldn't watch dispassionately.

It began with a scream that seemed to split Marcus right down the center of his being. So like his mother's scream. And again he was ten years old, impotent to help her, so frightened he was unable to even try.

But then he saw the men—young men, several wielding blades—crowding closer to a woman whose back was pressed to the far wall in a dead-end alley, and he snapped out of the momentary flashback.

The old rage, though, remained. The same rage he'd felt years ago and been unable to act on. Now he didn't think, he just moved. The terror-stricken woman huddled, wide-eyed, while Marcus kicked the hell out of her would-be attackers. Six of them. Four went down, two ran off.

Marcus stood there a moment, slightly amazed. He'd frankly expected to get his ass kicked. It was the first time he really understood just how powerful he was compared to other men. They couldn't fight their way out of a shoe box. He wasn't even winded. All thanks to Caine.

Shaking his head, Marcus turned to the woman and took a step toward her. But she suddenly shifted her gaze and pointed past him, babbling something incoherent.

Marcus sensed the movement, started to turn, caught what was happening from the corner of his eye. One of the men he'd put down was getting up. He had a gun and was lifting it, aiming it at Marcus.

Marcus spun the way Caine had taught him, but he knew there was no time. Then two things happened at once.

The gun went off.

And a man dressed in black, wearing a fedora with an unusually large rim, lunged out of the shadows and into the path of the bullet.

The man in black jerked, then crumpled to the ground. Marcus finished his motion, kicked the assailant, sent the gun sailing, kicked the man again and knocked him cold. Then he bent over the fallen hero.

"My God," Marcus whispered. "You're real. It's true. You're…the Guardian."

The hat brim bobbed with the man's weak nod. "That's right, Marcus. I am."

Marcus felt his heart stop in his chest at the familiar voice. "Caine?" Gently, he lifted away the hat. It was. His own mentor—the Guardian. "B-but…how? Why?"

Caine's face contorted in pain. "Take me home, son. There's a lot you need to know. Not much time, I'm afraid."

"But—"

"Take me home, Marcus. Take me home."

"I wasn't the first."

Marcus sat beside the bed. The doctor had come and gone by now but he'd said there wasn't a thing he could do. The strongest man Marcus had ever known was dying. And yet Marcus thought he'd never really known Caine at all.

"The first took me in when my parents were killed. He trained me, raised me. When he retired, I stepped up to take his place as Silver City's Guardian."

"Why?"

Caine wasn't in pain. Thank God. The doctor had given him something to take the edge off. But he'd refused to be overly sedated. Said he had things to say, things to see to, before he went.

Caine shrugged then, in that way he had, not just with his shoulders but with one eyebrow and a slight cocking of his head. "Had a score to settle. Criminals took away my life. I wanted payback. But it was more than that, Marcus. Some men...just aren't cut out for that other kind of life. I liked the solitude, the protection of secrecy. The anonymity. It was..."

"Safe," Marcus said.

Caine nodded. "I was on my way to help your family that day, Marcus."

Marcus's head came up, and he supposed he looked startled.

"Graham...he has ways of finding out things. Computers, connections. He got a tip about the hit, and I was on my way. But I was too late. By the time I got there it was over. I was devastated. My first failure, and I felt solely responsible for your family being killed. I wandered in the night, alone, miserable, and then I spotted you. And I knew immediately who you were."

Marcus nodded.

"It was meant to be, I think. I took you in, trained you. Now…now it's your turn, Marcus."

"My turn?" He stared at Caine with wide eyes.

"Everything I have is yours now. My wealth. The estate." He nodded at the rack near the door. "The coat and the hat. The identity."

"B-but…I'm not ready."

"Yes, Marcus, you are. Graham will help you."

"I can't…" Marcus shook his head, terror filling him. He could never fill Caine's shoes. Never. Caine was the greatest man he'd ever known. How could he even try to live up to such a legacy?

"I'm counting on you Marcus. It's my dying wish. Promise me you'll carry on in my place."

Marcus closed his eyes, lowered his head. "All right. I promise. I'll do my best, Caine."

"I know you will, son. I know you will."

One

Texas
December, 1998

There had always been secrets behind Laura's eyes. Casey Jones was born a snoop, and she'd die one. She'd spotted the shadows haunting the little girl right away, the very first night her parents brought Laura home and introduced her as Casey's new sister. Those shadows had faded in the more than twenty years since. Or they had until recently.

Lately, Casey had seen that haunted look creeping into her sister's eyes again. And she didn't like it.

Laura sat on the big brown sofa in the house where they'd both grown up, the house they still shared, reading this week's issue of *Lone Star*. But every once in a while she'd look up, huge dark eyes darting toward the door in response to some little sound. Or she'd get up and wander to the window to part the curtains and peer out before returning to her reading. She kept pushing her shoulder-length raven hair back with one hand, a sure sign she was nervous.

Casey watched her sister closely as she delivered the coffee and doughnuts she'd promised and took a seat beside her.

Laura laid the magazine down on the coffee table, atop a stack of others, and reached for a steaming mug. "Great column, Case," she said, ignoring the doughnuts. "Did you have to pay that hooker a lot to tell you about her liaisons with Senator Stewart?"

"Not a dime," Casey said. She grabbed a glazed, cream-filled concoction and inhaled the scent. "She couldn't wait to talk to me."

Laura finally faced her, a carefully cheerful expression pasted on her face. "Don't you feel kind of mean, exposing him that way?"

"Hey, at least I didn't publish the pictures." Casey shrugged. "Of course, if I had, they'd have had to sell this week's issue in the porno shop out on Gilmore Street."

Laura smiled. It was the first time in days. "You love this, don't you. Digging up secrets. Telling them to the world."

"I only tell the secrets that need telling," Casey said. She set the doughnut down and put a hand over Laura's. "I'd never tell yours."

Laura averted her eyes a little too quickly. "I know you wouldn't...not that I have any."

"Laura, when are you going to tell me what's going on with you?"

Laura pushed one hand through her hair again and closed her eyes. "I don't know what you're talking about, sis."

"Look, I know, okay? I've always known."

Meeting her eyes, Laura frowned. "Known what?"

"Well, for starters, your name isn't Laura. Or at least...it wasn't."

"Don't be—"

"Come on, it took almost a year before you got used to it or answered right away when someone called you."

Laura shook her head. "I was a little girl in a new place. It just took time to get...oriented."

"It was more than that."

"Let it go, Casey."

"I can't let it go." Turning so she faced her sister on the sofa, Casey gripped both Laura's hands. "I know you better than anyone in the world, Laura. We've been joined at the hip since Mama and Daddy brought you home to be my sister, and since they died, we've become even closer. Honey, I couldn't love you more if you were—"

"I know." Laura closed her eyes, and Casey saw the dampness gathering on her ebony lashes. "I know, Casey."

"Lately you've been acting...odd," Casey went on. "Scared. You're starting to get that same look in your eyes that I saw when you first came to us. What's wrong, Laura? What are you afraid of?"

Laura shook her head, saying nothing.

"In the car on the way home, you kept looking behind us. Is someone following you? Is that what this is about?"

Drawing a deep breath and blowing it out, Laura nodded, just once. "I...thought so. But it was just my imagination, Casey. Really, just drop this. There's nothing wrong."

"You know me too well to think I can do that."

Laura reached for a doughnut, took a big bite and

snatched up another magazine from the pile. Her signal that the subject was closed. But Casey wouldn't let it go that easily, and she figured her sister probably knew it. She'd get to the bottom of this with or without Laura's cooperation.

"Have you seen this yet?" Laura asked, holding up a copy of the glitzy *Prominence Magazine.*

Casey glanced at it and pursed her lips. "I only read news magazines."

"Well, this *is* news, sort of. They've been listing the world's most eligible bachelors, one a month since September. Mr. December is...interesting."

"Yeah? What, some rock star?"

"Not even close." Laura shoved the magazine into Casey's hands. An effort to distract her from the subject at hand, Casey knew, but she glanced at it all the same.

There was no photo. Just a sketchy drawing of a shadowy figure with a hat pulled down over his face and a long dark coat. The caption underneath the illustration read, "Elusive, mysterious, a modern-day hero—the Guardian has men curious and women panting."

Frowning her distaste, Casey couldn't help but read on. She got so involved in the story about some supposed vigilante who haunted the streets of Silver City, New York, rescuing people in trouble, that she ate two more doughnuts without even being aware of it. She read the last part aloud.

"Witnesses describe him the same way. A shadow among the shadows. A dark-coated man who appears out of nowhere, saves lives and then vanishes again without a trace. Female witnesses to the elusive Guardian's heroics tend to embellish a bit more, calling him tall, broad-shouldered and lean. 'He moves like a dancer,' one woman sighed. 'Yet with such incredible power and speed it's as if he's superhuman.' Another witness remarked that his eyes 'flashed like chips of gleaming onyx' when they met hers.''

"Pretty sexy, huh?" Laura asked.

Casey blinked up from the magazine, gave herself a shake and then grimaced. "It's ridiculous. An urban legend. You can't think this guy is for real."

Laura shrugged. "Maybe he is. Who knows? Too bad we don't have one like him here in Texas." She ignored her sister's exasperated sigh and got to her feet. "Let's go shopping and then go out for dinner, Casey. I'm in the mood for pizza."

Casey glanced down at her sticky fingers. "I shouldn't eat for a week."

"Oh, come on. For me?"

Laura's big dark eyes were irresistible, and Casey smiled and nodded. "For you? Okay, but you get the blame if I can't get my jeans buttoned tomorrow."

She'd do anything for Laura. Anything. And Laura knew it. It occurred to Casey that maybe that was the problem. Laura knew that if she told Casey what was really going on, Casey would try to fix it. No matter the risk.

And she was right.

* * *

When they returned from the pizza place in town, Casey stepped inside, snapped on the light and froze as a bubble of panic rose up from her belly to her throat. Laura came up behind her, glanced over her shoulder and gasped.

The house had been trashed. Drawers opened, articles scattered on the floors, cushions yanked from the sofa and chairs, even photographs taken from the walls and flung carelessly aside.

"My God," Casey whispered. Laura tried to push past her, but Casey held her back with one arm. "No," she whispered. "They might still be here. Let's get back to the car…quietly."

But when she turned, her sister wasn't moving. She was staring through the open door at the mess inside, and there was terror in her eyes. "Laura? Come on, we have to move."

Laura shook her head. "He's found me," she muttered, not blinking, though tears brimmed in her eyes. "Oh God, he's found me."

"What are you talking about? Who's found you?"

Sniffing, Laura clamped her lips. Casey gripped her shoulders and shook her gently. "Talk to me, Laura. What the hell is going on?"

"I c-can't."

"Come on." Casey maneuvered her sister back to the car, got the two of them inside and locked the doors. She picked up the cell phone even as she was backing out of the driveway, and by the time they'd driven a safe distance from the house, she had the local police on the way. She set the phone down, pulled the car to the roadside and faced her sister.

"Enough is enough, Laura. It's time to tell me everything."

Lifting her chin, Laura met her eyes. "No, Casey. I can't. Don't ask me to."

"I'll find out anyway."

"It won't matter."

"What the hell is that supposed to mean?"

Laura brushed tears from her eyes, but more came to replace them. "I...I'm going to have to go. Leave here, Casey. I...it's the only way."

"What do you— Leave here? Leave *me*?" Casey's mind jumped from one explanation for all of this to another, but it kept coming back to one screaming truth. "I can't lose you, Laura. God, you're all I have...in this world you're all I have."

"Me, too," Laura said, and then she fell into Casey's arms, sobbing. Her face pressed to Casey's shoulder, her tears wetting the silk blouse. And Casey held her close, stroked her hair and made promises she had no idea how to keep.

"I'll make it okay, I promise. You don't have to leave, Laura. Listen, just give me some time, okay? I'll find a way to keep you safe. I swear I will. I swear."

Laura sat away slightly, staring into Casey's eyes. "I don't want you getting involved in this."

"I know. I can protect you, though, without getting involved. I can, I know I can. I'll find a way."

Sniffling, Laura nodded. "Okay. Okay, we'll try it your way."

Relief rinsed away some of the tension. But not nearly enough. "We'll talk to the police, then, for tonight, we'll stay in a hotel. I've got to think, and you'll be safe there. Okay?''

"Okay," Laura said. She wiped her eyes dry. "Too bad we couldn't call on that...Guardian character, huh?"

Casey tilted her head to one side and reached out to swipe away a tear her sister had missed. "Yeah. Too bad."

Ridiculous idea. Silly. The guy wasn't even real...or probably wasn't. And if he was, he could be no more than some mercenary type or a self-appointed vigilante. And probably half-nuts to boot. What sane man would run around in a disguise? She was surprised he didn't wear a cape and tights, for God's sake.

But what if he was for real? What if...? He'd be the perfect choice to help Laura out of this mess. A shadow, a man who went unseen but was there to spring into action when the need arose.

She wondered how a person could go about contacting a shadow...if a person was so inclined, which she wasn't, of course.

He wouldn't have a listed number. Especially if he detested publicity as much as the article claimed. He was supposedly so elusive no one had ever so much as glimpsed his face, not even the people he helped, despite the love-struck woman's description of his onyx eyes. The trick, Casey decided, would be to get his attention.

Then she smiled slightly. "If he is for real," she said, thinking out loud, "I'd hate to be around for his reaction when he sees that article."

* * *

"What the *hell* is *this!*" Marcus threw the magazine across the foyer. It sailed ten feet, then slid several more over the smooth marble floor.

"I've no clue where they got the idea, Marcus, but what's done is done." Graham's face remained as stoic as always, but Marcus suspected he was also mildly amused by the Guardian's newfound celebrity. And that only angered him more.

"It's ludicrous! Do you have any idea the damage this kind of publicity could do?"

"Quite frankly, sir, no." Marcus gaped at him. Graham only lifted his brows slightly and went on. "The article says nothing about you that wasn't already known."

"The article," Marcus said, "is running in a national magazine. It's putting an unwanted spotlight right into our faces, Graham. I'm surprised this place isn't crawling with tabloid reporters already." He headed for the nearest window to peer out but saw only the serene, rolling lawns and the impenetrable iron fence beyond them.

"How could it be?" Graham asked calmly. "The piece doesn't say where you live."

"No, but every gossipmonger from here to L.A. will be doing his damnedest to find out."

"I never realized the full strength of your aversion to the public."

"Yeah, well, you do now."

"Indeed. It borders on the obsessive."

Marcus jerked away from the windows, glancing at Graham's face. But as usual he couldn't read it, didn't have a clue whether the old man was joking or dead serious.

"If my identity is discovered, Graham, I'll have to give it up. The Guardian can't function in the light, you know that."

Graham lowered his head for a brief moment. "Perhaps…that wouldn't be such a bad thing."

Narrowing his eyes, Marcus studied him. "How can you say that? It's my life, Graham. Just the way it was Caine's life, and his mentor's before him."

Shrugging his narrow shoulders, Graham still didn't meet Marcus's gaze. "You aren't like them," he said, so softly Marcus could barely make out the words.

"How am I different?" he asked.

Drawing a deep breath, Graham stiffened his spine, and when he lifted his eyes to Marcus's, the same old emotionless mask covered his face. "Never mind. You should go, Marcus. You'll be late."

Startled, Marcus glanced down at his watch. Late was not tolerable. Late could mean someone's life. Graham held the dark coat up, and Marcus shoved his arms into it. Like armor. Like a protective shield. Graham handed him the hat, a black fedora with a large brim. Marcus dropped it atop his head and gave the brim a tug, so it dipped, shadowing his face. And instantly he felt stronger, safer. Invincible. He tied the coat's belt, flipped up the collar and stepped outside, instantly blending into the darkness, the shadows. This was his world. It was where he wanted to be.

The tip had come via the Internet. Graham believed it to be valid, and he was rarely wrong. A property owner would burn his own warehouse tonight and try to collect a hefty check from his insurer tomorrow. The fact that homeless people slept in that warehouse didn't seem to have any impact on his scheme.

The Guardian would.

Marcus slipped through the shadows of the decrepit buildings along the waterfront. Waves lapped lazily at the shoreline. The occasional groan of a docked freighter and the whisper of a breeze were the only sounds except for the lonely echo of a distant ship's horn. The warehouse in question stood a few yards from him, listing slightly to the left. The place smelled of fish and seaweed and engine exhaust. Marcus would have to cross a wide section of pavement to reach the warehouse. There was no cover.

No matter.

He stayed hidden, watching, until he was sure no one was around. And then he stepped out.

Where they came from, he never knew. But suddenly cameras were flashing and a man was rushing toward him with a microphone in his hand. Marcus whirled, shielding his face and putting his back to the reporters, but one foolish photographer blocked his path. Camera in hand, the man loomed before him, aiming the weapon that would destroy the Guardian and preparing to shoot. The reaction was instinctive and unavoidable. Marcus's leg flashed up and out, and the camera sailed from the man's hand while he yelped in pain. When he bent over, injured hand pressed to his belly, Marcus raced past him, taking to the shadows once more. But this time, it was with a pack of journalistic hounds in hot pursuit.

He ran, he dodged, he used every trick Caine had taught him, and finally, breathless, he leaned against a brick wall in a part of the city he didn't know. He swiped the sweat from his brow, closed his eyes and listened to his heart thundering in his chest. More from anger than exertion.

The fools! How was he supposed to protect the people of this city if the press insisted on setting him up with phony tips and ambushes? What was he going to do the next time he had word that someone was going to be hurt or killed? Walk into what might very well be another trap? Or stay safe behind the walls of the estate and risk an innocent citizen dying because of his caution?

"Damn," he muttered. "What the hell choice do I have?"

Graham told him what choice he had the next night, after yet another setup where he'd very nearly been mauled and photographed by a mob of hungry reporters.

Marcus, sweaty, filthy and furious, had stripped off the coat and hat and collapsed on the sofa. He sat there, head tipped back, staring at the ceiling and wondering how the hell he could do the job Caine had asked him to do, when every time he stuck his head out the door, someone tried to snap a picture of it.

A cool, dewy glass pressed against his palm, and he glanced down. "Scotch, rocks," Graham said. "You look as if you could use it."

"I sure as hell could." Sitting up slightly, Marcus

swallowed the drink in one gulp, grimaced at the burn of it searing his throat and spreading in his chest, then held the glass up. Graham, anticipating his needs as he always did, had the cut crystal decanter in hand and poured more liquid amber over the ice.

"Another ambush?" he asked.

Marcus sipped the drink slowly this time. "Another ambush. And I don't know how the hell to deal with it." He glanced up at Graham's wizened face. "Did anything like this ever happen to Caine?"

"No, sir. I can't say that it did."

"Damn reporters. They want to destroy the Guardian so they can feed on his rotting flesh. Freaking carrion crows, that's all they are."

Graham lifted one brow and said nothing.

"I don't suppose you have any suggestions for me, do you, Graham?"

"Actually, I do."

Marcus waited. Graham walked to the wet bar and replaced the decanter of Scotch, saying nothing. "Well?" Marcus asked. "What is it?"

Graham took a piece of paper from the counter and turned. "I would suggest we leave Silver City. Give things time to calm down. Allow the reporters to find some other...flesh to feed upon, as you so colorfully put it."

Marcus blinked. Leave Silver City? And go where? God, he'd never been out of...well, he had, but that was when he'd been a kid, back in the life he didn't really remember.

No, he couldn't leave here. He was safe here.

"Where would we go?" he asked. "Just for the sake of argument."

"Texas," Graham replied without missing a beat.

Something flickered in Marcus's brain. Something blinding but too painful to be considered. He shook the sensation and the blurred memories away. "Why Texas? What did you do, spin the globe and point?"

Graham smiled slightly and handed the paper he held to Marcus. It was the personals section of the *Silver City Times,* and one of the ads was circled in red. Marcus read it aloud. "Guardian tired of solitary existence. Seeking wi—" His jaw dropped. "Seeking *wife?*"

"Indeed," Graham said. "Apparently you've taken out an ad, and you're asking that applicants reply to a voice-mail box at the paper."

"For the love of—who the hell—"

"I've checked into it already. The ad was purchased by a young woman by the name of Casey Jones, from Texas. So far, I, er, have managed to get an address and a telephone number for her, but I assumed you'd rather take care of this in person."

Marcus scowled at the ad. He didn't like leaving the seclusion of the estate. Had never enjoyed interacting on a personal level with the outside world. However, his privacy was being threatened here. Invaded. And without it, without his anonymity...

"Texas is far enough away to give the press here in Silver City time to focus on something else." Graham shrugged. "If we stay long enough, they may move on to *Prominence Magazine*'s next choice for world's most eligible bachelor."

Texas. It was there, lurking in the dark spot in the back of his mind that he never explored too deeply. Where the memories he'd lost or deliberately misplaced were alive and waiting like paper-covered packages to be unwrapped.

He hated Christmas. Hated presents. Didn't want the memories. After all these years he was quite content to leave them stacked beneath the pine tree in his mind, their wrapping never to be torn.

And yet Texas…it lured him, tugged at him. Maybe it was just his curiosity, or maybe it was something more that made him want to go there. To find what awaited him.

"Book us a flight, then," he told Graham, ignoring the older man's surprised expression. "We'll find out what this woman is up to and see to it she thinks twice about trying anything so foolish again. And in the meantime, we can take some much needed R and R…away from Silver City."

Graham nodded and reached for the phone. Marcus battled a cold shiver that danced through his bones. He felt danger. Like the light of day trying to penetrate his haven of shadows. If he stayed, he faced the press and their traps. If he left, he faced the unknown. Either way, it seemed a strong wind was trying to blow his long dark coat from his body and his wide-brimmed fedora from his head so the sun could shine down full on his face.

He wouldn't let that happen. Couldn't let it happen.

The shadows were where he lived. Alone, in darkness.

Solitude was free of pain.

Darkness…was safe.

Two

Casey was in her car when she got the call. And at first it scared the hell out of her.

"Casey Jones," she said, answering the phone just as she always did and managing to pass a slow car in the fast lane at the same time.

"You've made me very angry, Ms. Jones. I'd like to know why."

The voice itself was what got to her. And her reaction to it was instant. An unexpected chill, almost delicious it was so intense. That deep, rich tone spoke of secrets. Of forbidden pleasures. Of heat. It made her stomach clench tight, made her lick her lips—even as it frightened her in some foreign, primal way she didn't understand.

And then the words he'd spoken sank in, and Casey shook herself. What was wrong with her? Her home had been broken into, ransacked. Her sister was being followed for reasons she refused to explain, and yet Casey was getting turned on by strange voices over the phone.

She cleared her throat. "Who is this?"

"Do you make so many people angry every day that you can't guess?"

The Guardian. It had to be. It was exactly the way

she'd imagined he would sound. Dark, lonely, elusive. Sexy as hell. "Actually, yes," she said. "I tend to make a lot of people angry. But only when I have good reason."

"And what, exactly, was your reason for telling the world that I was in need of a wife?"

She released a long, slow sigh and felt her eyes widen just a bit. "Then it *is* you."

His sigh wasn't wistful as hers had been. It was impatient. "Your reasons, Ms. Jones?"

She ran a stop sign, heard someone blow their horn long and loud and veered sharply just in time to avoid being broadsided. "Damn! Hold on a minute." She pulled the car out of the intersection and onto the shoulder. "That's better. At least I won't get myself killed."

"I wouldn't be so sure of that."

She blinked. "Is that a threat? I thought you were supposed to be the good guy."

"Not to people who invade my privacy, Ms. Jones."

"Oh."

His breath filled her ear as if he were right beside her, and it sent a shiver down her spine. Every time he called her "Ms. Jones" in that deep, sultry voice, she felt heat sizzle through her. And she wanted to hear him say "Casey" in that same mysterious, almost whisper.

"Ms. Jones?" he prompted.

"Casey." She blurted it on impulse and instantly regretted that she had.

And then he said it, and the chills that ran up her

spine and into her nape were icy hot and delicious. "Casey." He breathed her name. Her eyes fell closed and she only popped them open again when he went on. "You were about to tell me why you took it upon yourself to place that ad."

She blinked. He was angry. She'd nearly forgotten all about that. "Right," she said. "Look, I'm sorry about the ad thing. I needed to get your attention, and it was the only thing I could think of."

There was a brief silence. Then, "You...you placed that ad just to provoke me into contacting you?"

"Hey, don't sound so skeptical. It worked, didn't it?"

His voice softer than before, he said, "I guess it did at that." But then it got hard again, even violent. "If you're a reporter—"

"I'm not." Casey bit her lip. It was a blatant lie. But it was obvious what this Guardian character thought of the press. If she told him the truth, he'd hang up and she'd never hear from him again. And she needed the guy.

"Then what *are* you after?"

She licked her lips, watched the traffic pass her by but didn't really see it. "I need your help," she said, very softly. "My sister is in trouble. Serious trouble."

He was silent a moment. "What kind of trouble?"

"I don't know exactly. She won't tell me. I only know someone is following her, and she's terrified."

"Are you certain?"

Casey bit back her anger. "She's my kid sister. She has fear in her eyes. There's a bond between us, and

I know her too well to mistake that look. God, didn't you ever have a sister?''

She thought he might have been taken aback, because he didn't answer for a moment. Then, clearing his throat, he said, ''Yes, as a matter of fact, I did. Once.''

Casey's heart tripped in her chest. ''I—I'm sorry.''

''I didn't mean, are you certain she's terrified. I meant, are you certain she's being followed?''

''Oh.'' She was focused on his voice now. Had there been pain there before? Had her remarks hurt him? Where was his sister now?

''Well?''

''What happened to your sister?'' she asked him.

He made an impatient sound that could have been clearing his throat or a deep growl, and she wasn't too sure she wanted to know which.

''If you want my help, answer my questions, Casey, and refrain from asking any in return.''

''That's hardly fair.''

''It's how I work. Now, what makes you think your sister is being followed?''

Casey frowned at the phone. ''Our house was broken into night before last,'' she said. ''They tore the place apart but didn't take a thing. So what would you say?''

''I'd say they were looking for something or they wanted to be sure you knew they'd been there.''

''At least you're not an idiot,'' Casey observed.

''If you thought I was an idiot, why did you go to so much trouble to get in touch with me?''

"I didn't *think* you were an idiot. Just feared you might be."

"Why?"

"Why? Well, gee, I dunno. Maybe I just jump to conclusions about guys who give themselves superhero nicknames and go around in hats and trench coats fighting for truth, justice and the American way."

He said nothing, and she realized she'd just insulted him big-time.

"That wasn't meant as a slam."

Silence.

"I apologize," she blurted. "Look, I have a short fuse, okay? And I'm really stressed out right now. I didn't mean anything by it. I need your help, here. The last thing I meant to do was insult you."

Very slowly, he said, "I didn't give myself the nickname. The newspapers did that. A long time ago. It wasn't even me then, and..." He let his voice trail off.

Casey's snoop muscle twitched. "It wasn't even you then?" She got that feeling in the pit of her stomach. The one that told her when she was on to something—close to uncovering someone's secrets. "What do you mean, it wasn't even you then?"

"We were discussing your sister."

The reminder was firm enough to get her back on track. And just insistent enough to make her file that feeling away in the back of her mind for future reference. The man hated being questioned, hated the press. Obviously he had major secrets to keep. And uncovering secrets was Casey's stock-in-trade. Her curiosity was aroused.

And it wasn't the only thing.

"So, are you going to help me protect her or not?" she asked him.

"I have to admit, I'm intrigued."

"Yeah, I'll bet. You need to get out of Silver City for a while, right? Give the press time to find another flavor of the month?"

"Why would you assume—"

"I read about your latest encounter with them in this morning's paper. They claim you assaulted a photographer."

"I barely touched him," he said, but softly.

"They're not going to leave you alone. I think you know that. So why not come to Texas?"

"It's not often I come across someone as utterly intrepid as you. Placing that ad was…"

"Placing that ad was ingenious," she said. "Let's cut to the chase here, okay? I'll pay you ten thousand dollars. Cash. Just say you'll come to Texas. Just meet Laura. I know if you take one look at her you'll want to help her out of this mess. Everyone who knows Laura loves her. Please, just—"

"I'm already in Texas, Casey."

She gaped. "You are? Where are you staying? Can I meet you so we can—"

"Actually, I'm not all that far from you. I've been watching you the entire time we've been talking. Nice car, by the way. I've always been partial to blue."

She blinked and craned her neck, examining the cars around her more carefully, searching for him, wondering what he looked like, what he drove. "Where are you?"

"You'll know that when I want you to know it."

"Oh, for crying out loud." She examined a wino on a park bench, dismissed him and continued scanning the traffic, the pedestrians, everything. "You've been paying too much attention to your own press, Mr.—er—whatever your name is."

"What makes you think so?"

"You sound as if you really believe this superhero hype they keep printing about you."

"Maybe I do," he said. "Maybe it's true."

"And maybe you're a lunatic. And maybe I'd better find someone else."

He paused, drew a breath. "You can try."

Closing her eyes, Casey knew she was out of time, out of options. "Are you going to help me? Just tell me yes or no, and stop with the games, okay? I don't have time for cat and mouse."

"To be honest, I haven't decided."

"Well, gee, do you have an idea when you might? I mean, with my sister's life on the line, I'm in a bit of a rush—"

"I wasn't being sarcastic."

"Then what were you being? Indecisive, or just deliberately cruel?"

He sighed heavily. "Wary," he told her. "I'm sure you can understand that, having read the papers. Or perhaps they didn't report the entire story. Maybe you don't realize that twice now I've rushed to the aid of someone supposedly in trouble, only to be ambushed by vultures."

Casey swallowed hard. "No," she said. "I wasn't aware of that." She glanced in the rearview mirror, saw a silver Infiniti Q45 pass by slowly. She was sure it was at least the second time that particular car had passed. She strained her eyes. Damn windows were tinted. She could see nothing beyond the dark silhouette of his head, the strong shape of his shoulders outlined in the dim, tinted glass.

"So you're wary," she said, running out of patience.

"Slightly."

"And you don't trust me."

"Not even a little bit," he said.

Casey sighed and shook her head. "So you're turning me down. Why didn't you just say so in the first place and save us both some time?" She put the car into gear, checked the mirror and waited for a break in traffic to allow her to pull out.

"I'm not turning you down."

She blinked at the phone. "You're accepting?"

"I didn't say that, either."

"You're not real good at decisions, are you, pal? Not much for clarity, either. You mind getting to the point?"

"If you'd keep quiet long enough, I'd be glad to."

She harrumphed into the phone, heard a deep chuckle on the other end, one that sent more shivers of awareness creeping over her nape and tickling at the base of her skull. She bit her lip, partly to keep from interrupting him again and partly in response to that sensation.

"I'd like to meet with you," he told her.

"Face-to-face?" She swallowed hard. "I thought no one had ever seen your face?"

"Let me worry about that."

She didn't answer. She was thinking, wondering. Was this guy safe? Was she out of her mind to be considering this?

"You'll be perfectly safe."

"Said the spider to the fly," she put in, still waffling. She needed him. But this was getting scary.

"You're the one who went to so much trouble to contact me, Casey. This was your idea, not mine. Believe me, luring attractive young women to dark places at night is not my idea of recreation."

Her throat went dry. "So you think I'm attractive?"

There was a pause. "Did I say that?"

"You trying to take it back?"

"No. It's true."

"I'd guess it must be easier to see through those tinted windows of yours from the inside than it is from the outside."

"Tinted windows?"

"On the Q45."

Again, there was a pause. "Very good, Ms. Jones."

"Casey, remember? So it's going to be dark? Where we meet?"

"Does that mean you're agreeing to it?"

It was her turn to pause, to think, to hesitate. "I guess I don't have much of a choice. When and where?"

She'd caught him by surprise. He didn't know the area. He hadn't been prepared for this. And usually he wasn't this indecisive or cautious. Then again, he'd never been through the things he'd been through in the days since the article had come out in *Prominence Magazine*. But there was more to it than that. His instincts were failing him today, and that rarely happened. Part of him was certain the woman on the phone was on the level. She wasn't making up the trouble her sister was in. There had been a slight wavering in her voice when she mentioned this... Laura's name. A change in tone. Her voice softened, trembled. And in doing so, touched off some strange reaction in him. An urge to believe her, to fix whatever was wrong.

Yet there were warning bells sounding in his mind, as well. A lot of them. Something wasn't right here. She was too sharp, too observant, too good at bantering with him without ever giving a thing away. She wasn't being entirely honest with him. About what, he didn't know.

But she was dangerous. He was certain of that. Dangerous...to him. How, he couldn't guess, but it was there. The knowledge, the awareness. She sent tingles up his spine with her voice, and when he'd driven past and glimpsed her behind the wheel, he'd felt more of the same. *Soft* was the word that came to mind when he saw her. Soft. The cloud of hair floating around her face. The size of her eyes. Big and brown and soft. She was right, he could see out through the tinted glass far more easily than anyone could see in. Then again, his eyes were honed to seeing what others missed. To seeing in utter darkness.

He'd seen her very clearly when he'd driven slowly past. And yet he'd been unable to resist driving by again, looking his fill, even though he knew that doing so increased his chances of being spotted.

"Mr....er, Guardian?"

Her voice, soft as the rest of her, came in his ear again, shaking him from his thoughts. He wasn't feeling sure of himself right now. He felt vulnerable without the protection of his fenced-in estate, the familiar security of Silver City and the anonymity he'd enjoyed for so long.

"I'm still here," he said.

"Do you know how silly that sounds? Mr. Guardian? It's ridiculous. If we're going to be working together, you'll have to give me something else to call you."

"We won't be working together, Ms. Jones. I work alone."

"We'll see," she said, and the words were laden with meaning. It made him uncomfortable. "So where are we meeting? And why bother, when you could just stop circling in your silver Infiniti, pull over somewhere and walk up to me?"

He almost smiled. She was clever. "I'm a mile from where you were parked," he said. "There's a park on my right, with a duck pond."

"Mulberry Park," she said.

"Mulberry Park," he repeated. "Meet me at the bench near the duck pond. All right?"

"Sure. I can be there in five minutes."

"Not now."

He heard her draw a breath, could almost feel her

nervousness coming through the line. "I was afraid of that. So...when?"

"Tonight," he said. "Midnight."

She groaned. Soft, almost erotic, that sound. He shifted in his seat.

"I suppose you're going to tell me to come alone."

He almost told her that coming alone wasn't all it was cracked up to be, but decided against it. "I'm afraid so," he said instead. "You have nothing to fear, Casey. I'm in the business of helping people, not harming them."

"Unless they're reporters who get in your way," she said softly.

He blinked. "You're referring to that report in the paper again, aren't you?"

"You did assault the photographer," she said.

"I was running for my life, and he jumped into my path and shoved a camera in my face. I didn't have much choice, the way I saw it."

She sighed.

"What? You sound disapproving."

"I don't know you well enough to approve or disapprove of you. It's just..."

"Just what?" At her silence, he found himself leaning forward in his seat. "Tell me. Oddly enough, I really want to know."

"You said you were running for your life," she told him. "But you weren't. You were running for your secrecy, to protect yourself from discovery. There's a big difference."

He nodded. She was sharp, insightful. "I suppose

that's true. Let's say then that I was running for my *way of life*. Which to me is the same thing.''

"Your way of life is that important to you? This secret identity of yours? Running around in the night thumping on bad guys? Why?''

Why? It was a question he consciously avoided. He'd heard his own mind whisper it to him more than once, but instinctively he ignored the question. Somehow, he knew the answers would be too painful to take.

With no more than a few words, she was poking around in the most secret places of his soul. He squirmed inwardly, wondering how the conversation had wound up here. "Are you going to meet me or not?'' He found part of himself suddenly hoping she'd refuse. Say no. Hang up and never bother him again. But mostly, he was praying she'd agree. He had to see her, talk to her, and he didn't even know why. For God's sake, *why?*

"Yes,'' she said. "All of a sudden I'm just dying to meet you.''

He didn't like the sound of that.

He didn't like the sound of that at all.

"A *date?*'' Laura stood with her hands on her hips, tapping one foot and looking at her older sister as if Casey had grown another head.

"Don't sound as if it's so far-fetched. It's not as if I never date.''

"It's *exactly* as if you never date. You *don't*, Case.''

"Do so.''

"Yeah? Name the last time."

"Eight months ago. Del Mason from the paper."

"Del doesn't count. You two only ate together so you could finish that article you were writing in time for the deadline."

"A dinner's a dinner."

"And Del is gay."

"So you're prejudiced now?"

"Prejudiced? I'm just saying gay co-workers don't count as dates!"

Casey blew a sigh. "Well, whether Dell counts or not is beside the point. I'm going out tonight."

"With who?"

"With a guy."

"Is he gay?"

Casey closed her eyes, brought that voice to mind again with no more than a passing thought and heard herself whisper, "God, I hope not." Her eyes flashed open. "Who the hell said that?"

Laura giggled. "You did. I can't believe it. You really like him, don't you?"

"Hell, I haven't even met him."

"So it's a blind date?"

"Very blind," Casey said.

"But very romantic. The duck pond at midnight? The guy sure has *something* on his mind. If I didn't know how good you are at taking care of yourself, I'd be worried."

"The point is, I'm not going unless I know you're safe."

Laura lowered her head. "I'm sick of hotels, Casey. I want to go home."

"Soon," Casey told her. "Just not tonight, okay? Please?"

"I suppose if I argue, you'll break the first date you've had in two years, won't you?"

"Damn right I will."

"Well, okay. I'll spend one more night at the hotel. For you. God knows I wouldn't want to be responsible for the longevity of your old-maidhood."

"Watch your mouth."

Laura grinned, crossed the suite that was costing them both a healthy portion of their weekly paychecks and sank into the leather sofa. "Now, tell me about him."

"There's not much to tell." Casey averted her eyes, wandering to the television stand to thumb through the *TV Guide* special holiday issue just for something to do. "I don't know him very well yet."

"Well, tell me what you do know. Is he gorgeous?"

"I think so."

"You *think* so? You mean you haven't even seen him yet?"

Casey shook her head. "He sounds gorgeous, though."

"Nice voice, huh?"

"Great voice."

"What's he do for a living?"

"Um..." Casey dropped the magazine, bent to pick it up again and straightened, banging her head on the stand. She rubbed her head, scowling. "He's sort of a public servant."

"Works for the government, hmm?"

"He's in…law enforcement."

"A cop?"

"He's more or less in…private practice."

"Oh, a lawyer."

"Let's drop this. I mean, it's only a first date. Not a big deal here."

"I can tell you're hoping it will be though," Laura said.

"You know me *so* well." Casey smiled through her gritted teeth. "Let's get some dinner." She wasn't the least bit hungry. In fact, the way her stomach was behaving, she doubted she'd be able to eat a thing. But it would help pass the time between now and her alleged "date." The park at midnight, indeed. She must be out of her mind.

"Okay, we'll eat," Laura said. "And afterward, I'll help you decide what to wear. We'll make sure you knock his socks off," she promised.

Casey suppressed a moan.

Three

It was dark. Damned dark. The duck pond lay like an oil slick, while its residents lined the shore with their heads tucked into their feathers. If Casey had half a brain she'd be doing the same—only the shore would be her bed at the hotel, and the feathers encased in a pillow. It was too dark.

Hell, she'd never *seen* it this dark.

She should have realized it would be. He wouldn't have suggested it without forethought, would he? No, not the elusive Guardian, a man who'd managed to keep his identity secret for all this time. He'd have taken the moon's phase into account even if it had never occurred to *her* to check a calendar. There was no moon tonight. And the stars did little but sit uselessly in the midwinter sky and twinkle. Lumination was not their thing.

She bumped her shin on the bench and hopped backward, swearing under her breath and rubbing the spot she'd no doubt bruised. At least she'd *found* the damned bench. Now if she could just find the guy who was supposed to be on it.

"Are you all right?"

She whirled when his voice sounded from behind her, then came to a halt and tried to breathe again.

He was only a dark shape, tall, looming so close she could feel the heat from his body. It was as if the night itself had taken on form, given itself a voice.

She tingled, told herself to stop it and tried to sound brisk. "You scared the hell out of me."

"I'm sorry."

"If you were so sorry you'd take me someplace with light. This is crazy."

"This is necessary," he said. "But if you'd rather call it off—"

"No. I'm here, let's get on with this." She strained her eyes in the darkness but could barely make out his shape, let alone see what he looked like. He was tall, too tall. She was on the short side, so she resented his height. She didn't like craning her neck to look up at people. Especially men who, in her opinion, felt superior enough without her helping them along by having to look up at them. He had nice shoulders. Wide. Powerful looking. His face was nothing but shadow. Shadow that moved when he spoke. She took a step closer, unaware of doing so until his hands came to her shoulders to keep her where she was. Big hands. But gentle. She went still when he touched her and tried to analyze the warm feeling pulsing in her skin where his hands were.

"Why don't we sit?" he suggested. And he took his hands away. Too soon. She hadn't figured out that feeling yet.

"All right." She turned, took a hesitant step toward the bench, then reached out with one hand, waving it back and forth in the darkness. Somewhere crickets chirped, and a chill breeze whispered across her nape.

She shivered, caught her toe on a piece of broken sidewalk and nearly fell.

And for the second time in as many minutes, he touched her. His hands clasped her waist and she sucked in a fast breath. What *was* that tingling sensation? Why did her flesh seem to come alive whenever his hands made contact? More important, was he aware of it, too?

"The bench is right here," he said, guiding her forward until she could feel the wood touch the fabric of the dress she wore. Had his voice been just a little unsteady? Slightly hoarse? His hands lingered a fraction of a second longer than was necessary before he took them away again. She didn't like this. All this…this *feeling,* as if the guy were giving off some kind of electrical charge. What did he look like? Suddenly she was dying to know.

She turned and lowered herself until she was sitting. But not relaxing. She perched on the edge, most of her weight on her feet, ready to spring up and run, should the need arise. Half-afraid he'd touch her again and jolt her right off the bench this time. Half-afraid he wouldn't touch her again at all.

"You're very nervous, aren't you?"

She nodded. Then remembered he couldn't see her. Or maybe he could. Maybe he was so used to encounters in total darkness that he could see like a cat. "I'm alone with a complete stranger in the middle of nowhere. You could be a maniac for all I know."

"And did you come prepared for that eventuality?"

"What?"

She heard him moving, felt his warmth as he sat down beside her, not close enough to touch her, but she could feel him as if he were. There was an intense awareness between them. Or maybe it was that power surge she'd felt when they touched—maybe she could feel it even without physical contact. Maybe just being near him was enough to make the hairs at her nape stand upright.

Or maybe it was just a natural reaction to being in the dark. The other senses heightening the way they did when one lost one's vision. Or maybe she was letting her imagination get out of hand here.

"You don't seem to me the type of woman who would come into a situation like this one unprepared."

She thought about the mace in her pocket. The little flip phone in the other. She'd put 911 on speed dial. "I took a few precautions," she admitted.

"Good. You'd have been foolish not to."

"So we've established I'm no fool. Have we accomplished anything else?" She was trying hard, maybe too hard. Being cute, being flip, trying to hide the tension that gnawed at her belly with this man. Trying to keep some semblance of control.

"Such as?" She didn't reply, and eventually he understood. "Ah, my decision."

"That's what this meeting was about, wasn't it?" He moved a little. She jumped, almost off the seat. Damn. So much for maintaining a cool demeanor.

He went still, and she could feel him studying her face, though she didn't know if he could see her.

"What can I do to make you more comfortable in this situation, Ms. Jones?"

She shrugged. "You can call me Casey. And...and give me something to call you besides Guardian."

"I can call you Casey," he said.

"But you won't tell me your name."

"My name is unimportant."

"Names are always important. There's power in words, you know. Especially in names."

"Is there?"

"You know there is. That's why you won't tell me yours."

"Do you think so?"

She sighed. The breeze picked up, blew her hair into her face. Then his hand was there, pushing it aside. His fingers were warm, strong. That shiver of awareness melted into her skin, and she closed her eyes, very nearly pressed her face closer to his touch. But then she realized what she was about to do, and opened her eyes wide again. "You can see me, can't you?"

"A little."

"You must spend a lot of time in the dark."

He said nothing for a moment. But his hand fell away, and she almost sighed at its absence.

"Tell me about your sister, Casey."

"All right." She had to pause a moment, gather her thoughts, recover from his touch. Imagine having to recover from someone's casual touch. She was in trouble here. But she lifted her chin, drew a breath. She could get through this. Deal with him. Figure out why he caused such odd reactions in her. She *could*.

"Laura...wasn't always my sister. My parents adopted her when she was six."

"I see."

"It wasn't something they'd talked about doing. There was no planning, no lead-up to it. They just brought her home one day. And I knew there was something more going on. Secrets they were keeping. It drove me nuts for a long time."

"You...dislike secrets?"

"Can't stand them. Never could."

"Sometimes they're necessary."

"I don't think so." She leaned back on the bench, looked up at the stars. "I think the truth is always better." She thought about the secret she was keeping from him. That she was a journalist, a reporter, and more than that, a reporter whose forte was revealing other people's secrets. Now, here she was, keeping secrets of her own.

"Why is that?" he was asking.

"Why is the truth better?" She narrowed her eyes on the dim silhouette of his face. "Because when you keep a secret, you live in constant fear of it being found out. You go over and over what might happen if someone reveals the truth." She shook her head. "I suppose you're right—sometimes it's necessary. But it's no way to live."

"You sound like the voice of experience."

She shrugged and said nothing.

"Do you have secrets of your own, Casey?"

"I might have one. A small one. Nothing like the bundles of deception you and my sister are carrying around."

He was quiet for a while. When she decided he wasn't going to reply to that, she went on. "I think this trouble she's in started back then, before I even knew her. Whatever happened to her before she came to us...whatever tore her from her real family..." She shook her head. "But I don't know that for sure. I only know she was scared then, and now she has that same look in her eyes."

"Where is she now?"

"Safe," Casey said. "At a hotel. We've been staying there since the break-in. But I'd really like to go back to the house. Laura would, too."

"You'll be able to do that soon."

She turned toward him quickly. "Will we?"

He drew a breath. It was deep and sensual, the sound of the night air filling his lungs. "You'll be safe there. I'll watch the house from outside to make sure of it."

"Then you've decided to trust me?"

She thought he might have smiled, but of course she couldn't be sure. "I've decided that you are telling the truth about needing my help. I'm still not sure I can trust you."

"But you're going to help me anyway," she whispered.

"Yes."

Of course he was. Who'd turn down ten grand just because of a little mistrust? "I'll have to go to the bank tomorrow. Withdraw the money. I suppose you'll want it in cash—"

"I don't want your money, Casey."

She blinked, tilting her head to one side and wishing she could see his face. "You don't?"

"That's not why I do this."

She realized she was gaping, snapped her mouth closed, shook her head slowly in wonder. "Then why do you? You intrigue me, Guardian. What kind of man lives in utter solitude just to maintain a secret identity that enables him to be everyone's hero? How did you end up where you are, anyway?"

His sigh was long and low. And his breath touched her face like a caress. "It's long, complicated...and private." He shook his head. "Besides, you wouldn't understand it. You have to live it to understand it."

"You could try me."

He got to his feet, stood towering over her and finally reached for her hands and pulled her up, as well. And then he looked downward, as if studying his own hands wrapped so intimately around hers in the night. "This meeting is over. I'll be at your house when you and your sister arrive tomorrow evening."

"But I won't see you, will I?"

"That's the way I work. And in this case I...I think it's for the best."

Then he *did* feel something—that strange energy surging when they touched. It was pulsing right now from their clasped hands. He must feel it...or did he?

He released her hands and took a step backward, and she realized that, elusive as he was, she might never get the chance to know what he looked like again. And she had to know...she had to. Impulsively, she lifted her hands and pressed her fingers to his face. He drew away fast, then stood very still.

"What are you—"

"Let me touch you," she said, and her voice came out softer than it ever had. "If I can't see you, let me feel what you look like, Guardian." She took a step closer, brought her hands up again, touched him, waited.

He didn't back away this time. "Casey, this is...this is not a good idea."

"It's only fair," she whispered. "You've seen me. At least let me have something to build on. So I can create a face for you in my mind. I need to picture something when I think of you, don't I?"

Her fingers ran across his forehead, smooth and warm. She traced his eyebrows and then ran her hands over the sides of his face, cheekbones, strong jaw, firm chin.

"You shouldn't be thinking of me at all," he whispered.

Why was he whispering? Was this as shattering to him as it was to her? As erotic? Was his heart beating faster? Hers was. She touched his nose, which was prominent and not quite straight, and his eyes, which were closed. And finally, she touched his mouth. Full lips, moist. They parted just slightly when her fingertips danced over them. And for just an instant the insane urge to press her forefinger between those lips assaulted her. To feel them close around it, sucking gently...

She drew her hand away, lowered her head, tried to calm her racing heart, catch her breath.

"Do you think you know me better now?" he asked her. He sounded a little breathless himself.

"Can you tell what I look like just by touching me, Casey Jones?"

"No," she said softly. "But I can tell what you *feel* like."

Marcus thought that if Casey knew what he felt like right now, she'd run all the way back to her car. He'd never been touched that way before. So intimately. So thoroughly, and with such devastating results. He wouldn't have been trembling more if he'd been having sex with the woman. Yet all she'd done was touch him.

He could still feel her. Her soft fingers roaming his face while he stood there, battling the urge to pull away, submitting to her examination without flinching. He thought she'd feel less afraid of him if he did so. But he'd had no idea the sort of reaction her touch would create in him.

He was attracted to her. Had been from his first glimpse of her in her car. But it was more than that now. She'd stood there with the breeze riffling her light brown hair, and she'd caressed him like a lover. And the part of him that wanted to draw away had done battle with another part of him. A part he'd kept in tight control all his life. The part that wanted to pull her closer. Touch her in return. All of her. Taste her. Feel the way she'd shiver in his arms.

She would. Because she was afraid of him. Drawn to him, too, yes, but afraid of him all the same. And it was a good thing to keep her that way, he realized. Because the woman was dangerous to him in more ways than he had at first understood.

So why had he just agreed to help her? Was he insane?

"Walk me to my car?" she asked him.

"Of course."

She turned in the direction of the parking lot, and he fell into step beside her. She stumbled, and his arm flashed out, his reflexes too honed to do otherwise. He put his arm around her waist, drew her to his side to keep her from falling. And she stayed there. He could see her. See the way she closed her eyes, bit her lip. She felt it, too. This pull.

"I'm going to break my neck," she said.

"I'll keep you safe." And he kept his arm where it was, walked with her tucked close to his side. Her thigh brushed his. Her hip. Her shoulder. Her hair moved with the breeze, tickling his face, and he inhaled its scent and writhed inside.

"Where did you tell your sister you were going tonight?" he asked her, because he had to say something to break the tension building in his groin.

She released a breath that was half laugh, half sigh. "I told her I had a blind date. Didn't know how right I was, did I?"

"She believed you?"

Casey nodded. Then, as if still thinking he couldn't see her, she spoke aloud. "She was amazed. I haven't had a date in…" Biting her lip, she lowered her head.

"It's been a while, I take it."

"Yeah," she whispered. "It's been a while." She lifted her head, looking blindly up toward his face. "How about you?"

He thought about his answer. "Socializing doesn't fit in with my life-style."

"That sounds like an excuse."

"Does it?" He led her to her car, almost sorry they'd reached it so soon.

"I...I guess I'll see you tomorrow."

"No," he told her. "You won't see me at all." Not if he had an ounce of common sense left, she wouldn't. He couldn't let this—this thing between them take over. He was in control, he had to remember that. He'd always been in complete and utter control—

No, Marcus, not always...

And nothing as trivial as a passing physical attraction was going to change that. Even one as intense as this one. He'd simply nip it in the bud. Refuse to allow it to enter his mind again. Keeping as far away from her as possible would make that a lot easier. Though...keeping away from her while keeping her and her sister alive was going to be a challenge.

She smiled, mischief in her eyes, sparkling up at him even in the darkness. "Don't be so sure I'll never see you, Guardian. Maybe I'll dive into my car right now and turn on my headlights."

"You'd like to," he said. "But you won't. You care too much about your sister to risk my breaking our deal and leaving."

She sighed, her smile dying. "You're right."

He knew he was right. And maybe that was part of the reason he'd decided to help her, even knowing that it might be the most foolish thing he'd ever done. That love he sensed in her for her sister made it impossible for him to refuse. It touched a chord deep within him. A painful chord, but a vital one.

She touched his shoulder. "Thank you," she said. "It's going to be all right."

"Do you think so?"

"I promise."

She smiled, and he could feel her relief. The burden seemed to ease from her shoulders. He could almost feel its weight settling onto his own. She gripped the door handle. Marcus turned away.

"Will we at least…talk again?" she asked.

"We'll talk," he told her. "Tomorrow."

And he walked away.

Four

Marcus returned to the suite Graham had booked for them, closed the door and leaned back against it. Damn. *Damn.* He'd told himself not to think about her, not to dwell on the sensations her touch evoked. But he'd battled those very thoughts all the way back here. It was foolish, ridiculous. Part of him blamed Caine. The man had taught him so much, educated him, trained him, made him into a sharp, strong fighting machine. But he'd never once talked to Marcus about this kind of battle. And Marcus had experienced nothing like this in his life.

He hated this feeling. His biggest asset, the thing that gave him the most confidence in his own abilities, was knowing that he was prepared for any situation he might be thrust into. And being prepared was the key to winning.

Well, he wasn't prepared for this. No one had trained him to deal with this. He didn't know any exercises or drills to hone his resistance. He didn't know a single weapon that would be effective against his own mind and body.

Maybe Caine had never experienced anything like this. Maybe that was why he'd never prepared Marcus for it.

"Feeling poorly?"

Marcus straightened away from the door and opened his eyes. Graham stood nearby, a cup of fragrant black coffee in his hands. As if he'd read Marcus's mind yet again. "No." He took the coffee. "Thanks."

"The case, then? Is that what's troubling you?"

Marcus shook his head, sipped the coffee and headed for an armchair. He was tense. His muscles tighter than a corpse in full rigor mortis. His neck ached and sent a dull throb up into the base of his skull. And for just a second he thought he felt something like fear flit through his soul.

Fear. Of what? A tiny mite of a woman? A woman who peered up at him, blind in the darkness, and made him feel as if she could see right through his flesh, through his disguises, through his secret identity?

Ridiculous.

"When will the computer system be set up, Graham?"

Graham returned to the sideboard and poured a cup of steamy tea from the silver service waiting there. "I should expect the equipment to be delivered late tomorrow morning," Graham said. "I can have it operational within an hour after that, give or take thirty seconds."

His dry wit reached past the veil of doom that seemed to be looming over Marcus's head, and he smiled at the older man. "Good," he said. "We need it." He sank into the softest armchair in the room and willed his muscles to relax. They didn't cooperate. "I think it's time you run a detailed background check on Casey Jones.'' He fished in his pocket for the slip of paper he'd scribbled on earlier and handed it to Graham. "See what you can find on her adoptive sister, Laura, as well. Especially anything about her birth family and the circumstances surrounding the adoption.''

"Those records are sealed, Marcus.''

"So are FBI files, Graham, but you've tapped into them on more than one occasion.''

"Yes, well…one can't have connections everywhere, can one?''

"What, you don't have an inside line with the stork? I'm shattered, Graham.''

"I can see that.''

Marcus stopped smiling, frowned instead. "What's that supposed to mean?''

"Just that I've known you for most of your life, and I can see that something has upset you quite severely this evening.''

Marcus sighed, lowered his head. "I wish Caine were here.''

"So do I,'' Graham said. "More often than you could believe. I never imagined he'd leave this world before me.''

There was such intense feeling in the words that Marcus forgot his own problems for a moment and searched Graham's eyes. But Graham quickly concealed whatever had been in them, and sipped his tea. Lifting his head again, his face inscrutable, he said, "Perhaps I can help with this problem, Marcus. I've been around a long time. I imagine I've learned a bit more than just how to run a computer in all these years."

Marcus's half smile came and went. There was nothing Graham didn't know about. Caine had hinted once that Graham had been an agency man. CIA. Or that was the impression Marcus had been left with. But in matters like this one, he honestly thought Graham was probably as uninformed as he was. Marcus sighed, lowering his eyes. "It's the client."

"Is it?"

He nodded toward the armchair opposite his, and Graham slowly crossed the floor and sat down in it.

"She's..." Marcus couldn't quite find the word.

"Beautiful?" Graham asked.

Marcus nodded. "Yes. But no more beautiful than a hundred other women I've helped over the years. And this never happened with any of them."

Graham didn't smile. But there was a suspicious twinkle in his old blue eyes. "What never happened?"

Marcus blinked, gave his head a shake. "I'm not sure. She...she's different. And there's something...very disturbing about her."

"Disturbing?"

Marcus nodded. Then searched Graham's eyes. "I sound like an idiot. But I'm telling you, Graham, this is very strange. I don't know how she's doing it, but she's making me..." He averted his eyes.

"Making you...want her?"

"That and more."

"But you've wanted women before, haven't you, Marcus? You've been with women before."

"This is different. Then it was manageable. I could decide how to proceed, whether to pursue, when to vanish again. This is...it's like she's wielding some kind of power over me."

"Ah."

Marcus snapped his head around. "What do you mean, 'ah'?"

Graham shrugged. "I've experienced this kind of thing before, Marcus. In my youth, of course."

"So what was it? What did you do about it?"

Graham's lips moved, stopping just short of a smile. "Her name was Emma," he said. "Oh, she had eyes like gemstones...and all she had to do was run her little finger across the back of my hand to reduce me to jelly." Graham shook his head. "I was a trained operative, specializing in high-risk covert activities. A tough guy, you know. It shook me."

"Then you *were* CIA."

"You know I can't tell you that."

Marcus sighed and settled back in the chair. "What did you do about it?"

Graham met Marcus's eyes, and his own were very serious. "Oh, the usual. Told myself she was trouble, vowed to stay away from her, insisted I could control the feelings the way I controlled everything else in my life."

"And then?" Marcus set his cup down and leaned forward.

"And then, boy, I married her."

He could have punched Marcus in the nose and startled him less. All this time...he'd never known.

He'd never once guessed. "Graham, I had no idea you'd been married!"

Graham lowered his head. "You...don't usually seem to enjoy discussing things of a personal nature," he said. "The subject never came up."

Marcus blinked and realized it was true. He and Graham had shared the same home for more than twenty years, and yet they barely knew each other. Not the way they should. Not the way members of a family knew each other. He had no idea where Graham went or what he did on his days off. Who his family might be. Where he came from. He'd only begun to suspect Graham's former career as a CIA agent from hints dropped by Caine on his deathbed when he'd seemed compelled to reveal all his secrets.

"You're right," he said at length. "I do avoid those kinds of conversations, don't I."

"It's quite all right," Graham said. "I fully understand why."

Marcus frowned. "That's fascinating to me, since I don't have a clue. Would you care to elaborate?"

Graham studied Marcus's face for a long moment. "No," he said. "No, I don't think I would." He set his cup precisely in its saucer and got to his feet, gathering up Marcus's empty coffee cup on the way past and disappearing into the kitchen.

Marcus stared after him and realized there was a lot about Graham that he didn't know. And for the first time, he was curious. But his tense muscles were not easing, even now, and he decided it was time he do something about that. "I think I'll head downstairs and try that hot tub," he called to Graham.

"Very well," Graham returned. "If you really think it will help."

There was no one else around. Which was nice. Marcus needed to be alone. To just sit by himself in the rushing, steaming water and let the tension ease out of him. Along with any and every thought that had to do with Casey Jones.

The hot tub was outside, in a corner near the pool, but with manmade rock piles stacked around it to give it a sense of privacy. There was a bar nearby. But it had closed long ago. Way too early, in Marcus's opinion. Technically, the pool and hot tub areas were closed, as well, but he ignored that. Best time to soak, the way he saw it. No one around. No threats to his solitude.

He took off his robe, laid it on a stone pile and walked down the steps into the hot water, into the steam. So much steam he could barely see out of it. Jets blasted the hot water so that it swirled around his legs, his thighs. He waded to the far side of the hot tub and lowered himself down, sighing the tension away as he did. Oh, this was good. If he had a whiskey in his hand it would be better, but it was damned near perfect. Almost as good as being back at the estate.

He shifted until a jet spewed a stream of heat right into the small of his back, and then he slowly relaxed. He tipped his head back against the far wall where the patio lights didn't quite reach and closed his eyes.

There was a change in the sound of the rushing water. A gentle swishing that hadn't been there before. Marcus brought his head up, opened his eyes and kept them open.

He couldn't see much through the steam, but he liked what he did see. A pair of legs that were short, but shapely, appeared on the tub steps. And then the body attached to them moved lower, slowly, like some kind of erotic tease show. Little by little she moved through the steam and into his line of vision. Her hips and the place where the black swimsuit crawled between her legs. Then her waist, her belly—flat and tight, but still covered up. He almost sighed in disappointment that the suit wasn't a bikini.

She said nothing, and he realized she must not even know he was there. No wonder. So much steam. A night chilly enough to keep the sane guests inside.

She moved farther down the steps. He saw round breasts with stiff little peaks. Yeah. A chilly night. There was creamy skin above the suit's curved neck-line. Cleavage. And then a slender neck, and a pretty little chin and soft brown hair, and...

His eyes flew wide and he went stiff.

Casey Jones stepped the rest of the way into the tub, still unaware of his presence. Dammit! She'd told him she and her sister were staying at a hotel. Why the hell hadn't he thought to find out which one?

She came toward him.

"Damn," he whispered. And he didn't even realize he'd said it aloud until she jerked in surprise, head coming up fast, wide eyes meeting his. Her arms flailed as she lost her balance. Her mouth opened, and then she toppled forward. He reached for her, but it was too late.

She landed with her head in his lap, face pressed tight to the front of his designer trunks. He had to bite his lip to keep from moaning out loud, even as she was struggling to get up.

He put his hands on her waist and helped her. Her head came out of the water, hair streaming, eyes blinking the chlorine away. She stared at him, her cheeks as red as apples.

"S...sorry," she muttered.

There was more light here than Marcus had first thought. Light from the lampposts scattered all around and from the tub itself. She could see his face. But, he reminded himself, she still didn't know who he was.

His hands were still on her waist. She was on her knees in front of him. As she tried to get up, she pressed her palms to his thighs, then realized what she was doing and yanked them away.

"Let me help you." He was careful to speak very softly, in case she might recognize his voice. He opened his legs and tightened his arms around her waist, pulling her closer but upward at the same time.

She blinked and stammered, "Thanks, um, I mean..."

She'd never have to know, he thought. She'd never have to know it was him. He pulled her closer, no warning, no hesitation, and kissed her. His mouth covered hers, worked her lips, pushed them apart, and then he tasted her.

She didn't resist. But she didn't respond, either. Except to shiver in his arms. Her mouth didn't move against his. Her arms didn't come around him. Puzzled, he ended the kiss, pulling back to search her face.

"You done?" she asked, her tone acid.

Marcus shook himself and wondered what the hell had come over him just now. "Sorry," he told her, and he let his arms fall to his sides.

She stepped backward, turned half away from him, then muttered, "To hell with this," and came whirling toward him again, fist first.

Her knuckles connected with his jaw and his head snapped back and sideways hard enough that he figured his stiff neck would be worse instead of better. Then she just stood there, glaring at him from furious brown eyes. "I came to use the hot tub," she all but growled at him. "And that's what I'm going to do. You can get out of here, or I'll report your little assault to the management and have you thrown out. What'll it be?"

He rubbed his jaw. Shook his head. "I said I was sorry."

"You're sorry, all right."

With a defeated sigh, he got to his feet and moved past her to the steps. But he felt her eyes on him, knew she was looking her fill, wondered if she liked what she saw.

"I had that coming," he told her, moving up the steps, reaching for his robe. "And to tell the truth, it's just as well. This would have been...a bad idea."

"Don't even think about coming back," she said. "I have mace."

He smiled unwillingly, and the action hurt his

wounded jaw. "I'll bet you do." He put on the robe. "Enjoy your soak, Casey. I won't bother you again."

"You'd better not," she snapped as he turned and walked away. He was all the way past the pool and going through the doors when he heard her yell after him, "Wait a minute! How did you know my name? Hey, you!"

He grimaced and picked up his pace, ducking around a corner and into a stairwell. He wiped his feet on the carpet so he wouldn't leave a wet trail, then took the stairs up to his suite.

Damn. He probably couldn't be screwing things up more if he tried. Then he rubbed his jaw again, smiling to himself. She was something, that Casey Jones.

Casey couldn't really enjoy the hot tub after that. She didn't like the idea of being alone out here while some kissing bandit who knew her name waited to pounce again. It had shaken her. And she supposed if she had to analyze it, it hadn't been a bad kiss. It was just that any kiss that was unwelcome was a bad one, so it was impossible to say for sure. The surprise, the fear made it impossible to know.

He must have been some kind of lunatic.

With a body like a god. But a lunatic was a lunatic no matter what he looked like in brief scraps of spandex.

She cut her soak short and headed back to her room. And in no time at all, she was able to put the hot tub incident and the man involved in it completely from her mind.

But she couldn't stop thinking about the mysterious

Guardian. *He'd* certainly had ample opportunity to pounce on her if he'd wanted to. But he hadn't. He was a man of too much integrity for something like that. Either that or he wasn't interested. But she kind of thought he was.

What if he had? What if he'd just grabbed her and kissed her the way that nutcase in the hot tub had done? How would she have responded?

She closed her eyes, tried to imagine it, then popped them open and chided herself for being charmed by the Guardian's mystique. It was just a cover. Who knew what kind of man he really was without the secret identity? Who knew what he even looked like?

She was going to find out.

She was going to learn everything there was to know about him or her name wasn't Casey Jones. She could do it, too.

The next day she spent her lunch hour ensconced in the local library's microfiche room, scanning back issues of the *Silver City Times* and printing up copies of every article that mentioned the Guardian.

The problem was, there were a lot of them.

She'd begun with recent issues and moved backward. But she kept finding more articles. December '89. July '85. May '80. And she kept going. September '75. August '68. February '55.

"Fifty-five?" She blinked at the screen, but there was no question. The date, the story, the Guardian. It was all right there in black and white. "Maybe he's just older than I thought."

But how old?

She kept searching. January 6, 1948. That seemed to be the first...the infamous story wherein the reporter had named Silver City's shadowy vigilante "The Guardian."

"Not that old," Casey whispered. She'd touched every inch of his face, and no way had that face been around in 1948, fighting crime. He'd have to be at least seventy years old to be the man in this piece.

Casey leaned back in the chair, closed her eyes, shook her head. "Two answers," she whispered. "Either he's immortal...or there has been more than one 'Guardian' over the years." He'd alluded to that, hadn't he? Yes, suddenly his words made more sense. "It wasn't even me then," he'd told her, referring to the time when the nickname had been given to him. She'd wondered then. Now she thought she understood.

The role seemed to be handed down...one generation to the next. But to whom? Was it a family thing or...or something else?

She narrowed her eyes on the screen as she hit the print key and waited for the final piece to be printed out. "And I don't believe in immortality, so it's obviously got to be the latter." She scooped the completed copies into a neat stack, tucked them into a file folder and stuffed them into her briefcase. Lunch hour was over. She'd be late getting back to work, but she didn't think anyone would question her. She worked through so many lunch hours that *Lone Star* owed her a year's worth. She was supposed to be working on a story.

Her journalist's blood flowed a little faster. Maybe she was.

No. No, she couldn't...

But think of the headline. Texas Reporter Succeeds Where All Others Fail! Identity Of The Guardian Revealed! Hell, it would go national. She'd probably end up entertaining offers from...

"Knock it off, Casey!"

She spoke harshly and aloud, drawing odd looks from the few other people in the room. A librarian and a pair of geeks. She shook her head and kept walking. The Guardian was helping her, helping Laura. And he'd refused to take any money for doing so. No, she wasn't going to repay that by plastering his precious secrets all over the front page.

What she learned would satisfy her own curiosity. Nothing more. Besides, she'd wasted an entire lunch hour digging up dirt on the Guardian instead of trying to find out more about her own sister's problems.

But there was the rub. She'd dug as deeply as she could into Laura's past, and she'd run into a brick wall. Solid brick. She'd tried every trick in the book and even called in some favors to get past it, but she'd gotten nowhere.

She'd researched mob bosses and secret service agents and had more success. It was damned *weird.*

Maybe *he* would have better luck.

She walked up the dark, echoing stairs into the main floor of the library, loving the musty-paper smell that filled the place. She thought back to the night before. To touching him and feeling the power of his reaction. Her stomach tightened, and a ball of longing formed there.

She ought to be ashamed of herself for feeling what she was rapidly believing to be desire—intense desire—for a stranger. But she wasn't. It seemed to Casey that she'd never had much choice in the matter. He was the one making her feel this way…somehow. It wasn't her fault.

She hated that he could be capable of making her want him while part of her was still afraid of him. And who wouldn't be? Shadowy figure, living in the darkness, never revealing himself to anyone. He was scary. She wasn't even altogether sure he was *real*.

But he *felt* real. Oh, damn, he felt so real.

Her face heated, and she had to brace her hand on the door frame, rest a minute, catch her breath. Like a hot flash, it rushed through her—a wave of this *stuff* she'd been feeling. It left her weak. Breathless. Dizzy.

Damn. "The man's like food poisoning," she muttered. Then she shook herself and went on her way.

The day dragged by. She worried about Laura, just as she did every single day. But Laura was safe. No matter how insane he might be, no stalker would make a move during broad daylight at an elementary school. First, this wasn't a small town. There were metal detectors and security guards at all the entrances. Second, you had to state your name, show ID and explain your reasons for visiting before they'd even let you inside that school. It was one of the safest in the state. And it was where Laura had been teaching kindergarten for the past five years.

So she was safe.

She was *probably* safe.

Casey reached for the phone on her desk and called her sister at work just to make sure.

The house was like some young girl's daydream. A simple two-story Cape Cod, white with black shutters. Picket fence. Flower boxes full of purple pansies. A neat sidewalk curving from the paved driveway to the front door, lined on both sides with marigolds.

He'd already been there for hours by the time the two women arrived home. He'd had preparations to make. The sensor at the back door that would let him know if anyone opened it. That had been easy, fast. A temporary fix. He'd gone inside, looked around. A lot more needed to be done. He'd have to talk to Casey....

The blue compact pulled into the driveway, and the two women got out. Marcus glimpsed the younger one, Laura, and his breath caught in his throat. He couldn't have said why. But Casey had been right. One look at her would have convinced him to take this case, even if he'd been determined not to. There was something about her...

Not the same kind of thing that attacked without warning when he looked Casey's way. Not that wild thing that had taken over last night and made him kiss her. This was far different. But just as powerful.

Laura looked like one of those sad child paintings he'd seen once. Huge dark eyes, welling with secrets. Jet black hair that was childishly unruly. Lips like a little girl's, full and bow-shaped. She was smiling, saying something to her sister as she got out and walked toward the house, but Marcus didn't miss the slight hesitation. The way she looked around her before opening the front door, glancing over her shoulder. Casey was right. There was fear in her eyes. And the look made him want to protect her. To make sure she was safe.

Some women seemed to elicit that kind of response in a man, he realized. But in this case, he didn't think it was that. He thought there was more to it. More, maybe, than he knew himself just yet.

He looked away from Laura as she entered the house, focusing on Casey instead. She got out of the car, locked it and then paused in the driveway, turning in a slow circle, eyes scanning everything around her. But when Casey looked around, it wasn't in fear. She was looking for him, he realized, and caught himself shrinking backward into the trees along the roadside where he stood. It didn't matter if she spotted him. Why was he acting this way?

With Casey, he didn't get hit by an urge to protect her. It was more like an instinct that he'd best protect himself.

And what was up with those clothes?

She wore jeans that looked way too good, and a cropped T-shirt that didn't quite meet them. So that her tanned waist played peekaboo with him every time she moved. He caught a glimpse of her belly button and then realized he was craning his neck.

He settled down and told himself to relax. To treat this like any other case. To forget the way her mouth had tasted, the way her body had looked in that bathing suit. The way she'd looked, like something exotic and supernatural, standing there staring at him in surprise, surrounded by ethereal steam and unearthly bubbles.

Oh, hell. It was going to be a long night.

Five

He was out there. She knew he was. He'd said he would be talking to her today, but he hadn't. He'd also made it very clear she would not be seeing him again. But she was going to. Her curiosity wouldn't ease. She couldn't let this thing go. She couldn't.

Nothing unusual went on in the house that night except that Laura's nerves seemed raw. She jumped at every sound. Casey almost wished she could tell her sister not to worry, that there was a phantom crusader out there in the darkness, standing guard. But that would only freak out her kid sister even more. Laura didn't want Casey involved. Didn't want her to know what was going on, much less drag some stranger into her private hell.

Of all the criminals she'd interviewed or written about over the years, Casey had never come across anyone as secretive as her sister.

Or she hadn't...until she'd met the Guardian.

She sighed. Secrets were dangerous. Why was she the only one who could see that so clearly?

Eventually, Laura went up to bed, though it was hours before Casey stopped listening to the soft sounds of her pacing. She crept upstairs and peered into her sister's room, only to see her sound asleep, with the lights on.

Good. It was time, then. Time to talk to this Guardian. He could protect Laura just as well from here as he could from—she parted a curtain and peered into the night—from wherever he was.

She walked from room to room, flicking off all the lights. Then she paused at the front door and extinguished the outdoor light, as well. Drawing a deep breath, she stepped outside. She walked a few steps along the sidewalk until she was certain he could see her. And then she just stood there. Waiting.

What the hell was she *doing?*

She stood there, hands thrust into the pockets of her faded jeans. The night wind played in her hair moving it this way and that like a set of adoring fingers. Marcus let his eyes travel lower. She was barefoot. Standing barefoot on the blacktopped driveway and waiting.

Waiting, he realized, for him.

No way. Bad idea.

But she wasn't moving. And if there *was* someone around here, someone dangerous, she wasn't safe just standing there in the open. She might as well hold up a sign. Drive-by Shooting Target: Aim Here.

He sighed. She'd leave soon. She'd have to.

"La-da-da-dee-dee." She hummed a tuneless melody, then added words. "I can stand here...*all* night."

"Oh, hell," Marcus muttered. She would do it, too. She'd stand there until he went to her. Stubborn little... Well, he couldn't just walk out there to her. Then the bad guys would know she'd found herself some help, and Marcus didn't want them forewarned. He slipped out of the bushes, crept through the brush all the way to the back lawn, then hugged the edge of the house, keeping to the shadows. He ducked into the narrow space between the house and the garage and crept along it until he reached the driveway. When he was a few feet from her, he stood watching her.

She yawned. When she did, she arched, lifting her arms slowly above her head and stretching. Her cropped T-shirt rose higher, revealing the curve of her spine, the tuck of her waist, her rib cage. Hell, any higher and...

He closed his eyes. "Casey," he whispered.

She went still, then slowly brought her arms back down again. "Where are you?"

"Back here," he told her. "Keep your voice down. And act casual."

She nodded once, careful not to look his way. Then she wandered a few steps away from him, kicked a pebble off the blacktop, turned and wandered as if without direction. She did the aimless amble very well. Eventually she stepped into the shadowy stretch of grass between the house and the garage. Too pretty to be called an alley. She had shade-loving shrubs growing here, and some night-blooming flowers that were already open and spreading their heady fragrance. The space left was only a couple of feet.

She came right up to him, stood toe to toe and tipped her chin up. Then her hand rose slowly so her fingertips could trace the brim of his hat. "You could have left the hat behind, you know. I can't see my own hand in front of my face out here."

"Good."

"So can I take it off for you?"

"I'll keep it, thanks." He covered her hand with his to move it away from the hat, but that was a mistake. The contact jolted him. He wanted to touch her everywhere.

She shivered when he held her hand, sighed when he released it, tried to hide her reactions by keeping a cool tone to her voice.

"I'll bet you're really ugly, aren't you?" she said. "Do you have an extra eye or warts or something? Is that it?"

She amused him. He liked her teasing, though he wasn't going to let her know it. Still, he smiled. She wouldn't know. She couldn't see him. Keeping any hint of humor from his voice, he said, "Did you feel any warts when you touched me last night?"

"No. But maybe I missed something...not that it would matter."

"Wouldn't it?"

She moved her head slowly from side to side. "I put very little stock in physical beauty, Guardian."

"And this should matter to me because...?"

"It does matter to you. And you know it."

"Do I?"

She nodded. "I don't care what you look like," she told him. Then she shrugged, lowered her head, dug her toe into the grass.

"Why did you make me come over here, Casey? Is there something wrong?"

She sighed. "Not one particular thing," she said, speaking slowly, giving him the distinct feeling she was making all this up as she went along. "It's...well, I couldn't see you. I needed to make sure you were really here."

"I'm here."

"But will you stay?"

"I'll stay."

"How will I know? You could leave at any time, and I'd never know it. And my guard would be down, because I'd think you were still out here. Someone could come in and—"

"I'll stay, Casey."

She lowered her head again. "I keep...hearing noises."

He narrowed his eyes on her. "And you're scared?"

"Yes."

"Liar." Her head came up fast. "You're not scared of anything, Casey Jones. So what's with this damsel-in-distress routine?"

She kept her chin up, and he imagined if she could have seen him, she'd have been meeting his gaze without even blinking. "I am scared of some things. Of losing my sister, mainly. I can't go to sleep because I'm afraid if I close my eyes something will happen to her. And if I do manage to doze off, I have nightmares about losing her forever. I can't..." She broke off, turning away. "I don't expect you to understand."

Impulsively, he put his hands on her shoulders. "I do understand, Casey. Better than you could possibly imagine."

"Then come inside."

He said nothing, went to move his hands away, but paused when one of hers came up to settle atop his larger hand where it rested on her shoulder.

"Don't let go," she whispered.

"Casey—"

"It's true, what I said. I am scared. I will feel better having you close by. But it's more than that, too, and I think you know it. I want you close to me."

"All the more reason I shouldn't—"

"You want it, too." She lowered her head, sighed softly. "I've turned off all the lights. Laura's sound asleep. You could guard us better from in there than from out here, anyway."

"Out here my mind is on what I'm doing."

"And in there it wouldn't be?"

"You know damned well it wouldn't be."

She turned slowly, rubbing her cheek over his hand as she did, and finally faced him again. "Come inside," she whispered.

"It's not a good idea."

"I can't sleep. I need to know you're there... close."

"Casey..."

"What if I promise you that nothing will happen between us tonight?"

He turned his palm so that it cupped her face, caressed her soft cheek. "If you let me in that house, Casey, it's anyone's guess what will happen."

She turned her lips into his palm, kissed him there. He sucked in a sharp, painful breath. Then, impulsively, he pulled her close to him. She gasped but didn't object, didn't pull away. He slid his hands underneath her T-shirt, running his palms along the warm, tight skin of her waist, her back, sliding around to the front and rubbing across her breasts while she cried out very softly.

"I've never wanted like this," she whispered, and the words were like gasoline on an open flame. "I don't even know you, can't even see your face, and yet I want...I want..."

"What?" He held her closer, and when her hips arched tight against him, he knew. He bent her backward, leaned over her, clasping her body tight to his, and kissed her. She opened her lips to let him in. Invited, begged silently for his tongue. He couldn't refuse, wanted to taste her as badly as she wanted to be tasted. So he probed, dipping his tongue deeply, stroking the inside of her mouth while his hands kneaded her backside. She trembled all over, and he did, as well.

And then a dog barked in the distance, jarring him back to reality. He straightened, still holding her, letting her get her balance. "This is exactly what I'm afraid of," he told her. "Losing control. Forgetting the job I'm here to do. You could distract a man, Casey."

She lowered her head. "I'm sorry. This isn't the way I normally behave."

"I know that."

"How could you?"

He said nothing. Casey shrugged, sighing heavily. "It won't happen again," she told him. "This is my sister's life we're talking about. I'm not going to risk it for the sake of some fleeting chemical reaction to a man I barely know."

He stared down at her, at the sincerity on her face. "Is that what this is? A chemical reaction?"

She took her time in answering him. "Don't... don't *you* think it must be?"

"I don't know. I haven't had much experience with this kind of thing."

"Hey, I'm not exactly the happy hooker myself, you know!"

"If you were, I'd know how to deal with all of this."

She made a face at him, shook her head. "At least I know it's not just in my head."

"It's not. But, Casey—"

"Nothing can come of it. I know. I mean, how can I not know? You won't even tell me your name."

"It's for the best," he said, but his voice was coming out oddly soft.

"Understood. It's all understood, Guardian. And now that it is, now that it's out in the open and we know where we stand, will you just come inside? I'll make coffee. We'll talk...just talk."

"All right. But only for a while."

"Only for a while."

She walked beside him to the back door, because it was more secluded from the view of any curious— or diabolical—onlookers. "Wait," he said, and took something from his pocket, a miniature remote control. He thumbed a button. "Okay, go ahead."

She was impressed. "Seems like you've thought of everything," she said. And then she opened the door and stepped inside.

He came right behind her.

The kitchen was pitch-dark, darker even than it had been outside. She was blind. Totally blind. And she shouldn't have stumbled, but she did.

He was quick to grab her hand. "Let me help you," he said in a voice barely above a whisper. "I can still see."

"Like a cat," she replied, and she felt his hand close around hers. Warm, strong, gentle all at the same time. That tingling awareness danced up her arm and made her go soft inside. She'd told herself she wanted to get him in here so they could talk, and maybe she'd drag something out of him about himself. Because she had to know. She had to know. But when he touched her, she realized she wanted more than just to know about him. A lot more.

He took her to the kitchen sink, anchored her hands on its edge and then moved away. When he came back it was with the coffee carafe. She felt it when he pushed it under the spigot and cranked on the faucets. "I know you promised to make the coffee," he said. "But I don't want the water poured down my shirt, so..."

"Very funny. I'm not a klutz...just not a bat like you."

He moved away and she heard him pouring the

water into the coffeemaker. Then he was back. "Where's the coffee?"

"On the shelf just above the pot. Filters, too."

She heard him moving around some more, then there was a click, and the coffeemaker started gurgling. He took her by the hand again and led her unfailingly through her own house to the living room and the sofa. "You seem to know your way around here pretty well," she said, already suspicious.

"I was here earlier today."

Of course he was. He'd installed some kind of contraption on the back door. But she hadn't imagined him *inside* the house.

"I had to look around. See where the weaknesses are, where you're vulnerable."

"Oh."

"I hope you're not angry."

She shrugged. "Apparently my locks aren't that good."

"Not for a professional." His voice came from yet another locale. She was swinging her head in a different direction every time he spoke.

"Will you sit down? You're making me nuts."

"Sorry." He sat down. Right beside her on the sofa. So close she could have easily tipped her head to the side and let it rest on his shoulder.

She licked her lips.

"You need dead bolts," he was saying, so absorbed in his job that he apparently hadn't noticed that he could put his arm around her with barely any trouble at all. Or blow in her ear if he wanted, with the merest crook of his neck. "You already know about the sensor I put on the back door, so I'll know any time it opens. But the windows need locks—''

"The windows *have* locks."

"First floor, yes. But the second-story windows don't."

"So you're expecting your cousin Spider-Man?"

He laughed. Soft, sexy. And then he leaned back on the sofa and released a breath. "You're cute as hell."

"Am I?"

"Yeah." He sat up a little, reached out to brush a wisp of hair from her forehead. "I like you, Casey Jones. You're tough, you're smart."

"And I'm cute," she said. "Don't forget that part."

"I'm not likely to forget that part." His voice was low.

She leaned back and closer to him at the same time, knowing he knew it and hoping he didn't mind too much. "How long have you been...you know, the Guardian?"

He was relaxed. His guard was down. And she was taking advantage. She knew that. But she couldn't help herself. She was so curious, so interested.

"For almost thirteen years now. I was nineteen."

Thirteen years ago. Casey's brain worked rapidly. That would mean in 1985 he was nineteen, so he was thirty-two now, and he was born in '66. Probably in or near Silver City.

She filed the information away, vowing to remember. Then she sighed. "So you aren't immortal after all."

"Immortal?" He glanced down at her, his face so close to hers she could feel his breath.

"Well, I did some reading about you before I contacted you. I mean, I wanted to be sure you were for real."

"And what did you learn?" His voice wasn't as relaxed anymore. It was wary now.

"Nothing to learn. It just seemed odd to me when I met you that first night that you weren't...older. I mean, the *Silver City Times* mentioned you way back in, oh, I don't know—forty-eight or something like that."

"Did they?"

She tilted her head. She was giving too much away. He was really suspicious of her now. She sighed and leaned against him. "It doesn't matter."

"Doesn't it?"

"Not in the least," she muttered. "Not to me. I'm just glad you're here. I don't know what I would have done—"

"You'd have done fine," he said softly. She thought a relieved breath escaped him. Thought perhaps his body's tension eased a bit. "You're resourceful."

"You think so?"

"The way you got me to contact you is proof enough of that," he told her.

"I've wondered about that again and again. What made you decide to help me after I pulled a trick like that?"

He shrugged. She was close enough now that she felt the movement. "I had several reasons."

Her hand touched his cheek. "Will you tell me what they were?"

He nodded. Shuddered. Gently covered her hand with his and moved it away. "I was intrigued. I wanted to meet the woman with the brass to try something like that."

"And that was all?"

"Oh, no." He sat a little straighter, putting a bit of distance between them. "There was more. There was...there was the fact that I'd have to come to Texas."

"You needed to get away from the Silver City press," she filled in.

"I think it might have been more than that. Something...something about Texas rang a bell in my mind."

"You've been to Texas before? Where?"

"I don't know." His voice was deadly serious. "Parts of my childhood are..." Then he caught himself, seemed to shut off the flow of words.

She sat straight, straining her eyes in the darkness. "You mean you don't remember?"

"I've said way too much." He turned his head.

"Something horrible happened to you, didn't it?"

He shook his head. "Don't ask me, Casey."

"You said something about a sister. A sister you lost. How did you lose her? Was she...was she killed?"

He was silent for a long time. Slowly, he said, "Suffice it to say, I know what it's like to love a sister and to lose one. And it's just one more reason I decided to help you."

Her heart stopped. Right there, on those words, it just stopped. And this time when her hands came to his face, he let them remain there.

"I don't know why I'm telling you any of this."

"Yes, you do," she whispered. "You know you do."

He shook his head. "It's not something I talk about."

"With me it is."

"That doesn't make any sense and you know it, Casey. It's only a chemical reaction between us. Right?"

"If that's all it can be." She straightened her fingers until they threaded into his hair, massaging his scalp gently. "Go on. Your sister…"

"She was…she was only four." The words seemed to spill from him without his permission. "Six years younger than me." He drew a shuddering breath and lowered his head. "She was killed. Our parents, too."

Tears pooled in her eyes, and she leaned closer to kiss his cheek. "It's all right."

"No, Casey." He removed her hands but held them clasped in his. "It's not all right. Never has been, and never will be. I've said way more than I should have. If you were a reporter, you'd have enough to nail me by now. But I thought if you knew, you'd understand why there can never be anything…"

"Between us? Between you and anyone in the world?"

He nodded. "I'm a loner. It's the way I like it, and it's not going to change."

Oddly, she no longer gave a damn about the information she was gleaning, the secrets she was learning. All she could think about was how it would have destroyed her to have lost her mom, her dad, and Laura, all at once. And how retreating behind a secret identity and leading a life of utter solitude was probably a fairly mild reaction compared to the one she'd have had, had it been her in his place.

And all she wanted to do right then was hold him and make it all right. But he'd erected a barrier—seemed to think that his telling her these things would strengthen the wall. God, he couldn't have been more wrong.

Then, as they sat facing each other in the darkness, a click sounded, and light flooded the room.

She saw him...but only briefly. Only enough to note the glistening of his lashes. And then he jerked her into his arms, hard and fast, pressed his mouth to hers and kissed her with everything in him.

''What the heck is going on down here?'' Laura asked in surprise.

Six

Her mouth was warm on his. Silken but firm. Subtly demanding. Confident...yet trembling. Marcus had been taken off guard, one minute horrified at his unmasking, the next kissing Casey in some misguided attempt to keep her from seeing his face. She would close her eyes and her sister would turn off the lights and retreat in silence. But it didn't work that way. He was under attack, even though he was the one who'd instigated the kiss. Emotional and physical attack. And it was every bit as dangerous as if she'd taken a swing at him or fired a weapon. Her response to his kiss made him reel. The passion of it, the honesty. He tasted tears on her lips, and something inside him shuddered. He didn't know how to react. His mind seemed to shut down, refusing to function. His eyes first widened, then went so blurry he had to close them. And even as he did, the shock faded. His breath soughed out of him and, amazingly enough, into her. She inhaled his sigh, drank it in, devoured it.

And he realized he was finally reacting. Oh hell, was he *ever* reacting. Her lips were succulent and undulating, parting and closing in a slow, hypnotic rhythm that *made* him react—made him move his mouth over hers, bury his fingers in her hair, pull her closer. The shock was gone. Desire was the only thing making his heart pound and his skin dampen now. Pure gut-wrenching, mind-blowing desire.

He'd never felt it before. He'd thought he had, but he knew right then that he hadn't. Not until the first time he'd kissed Casey Jones. If that first kiss had been a promise, this one was its fulfillment. No one had ever touched him until Casey Jones.

"Er, excuse me. I, uh, didn't realize..."

The sound of her sister's startled, still-sleepy voice was enough to remind him that he was doing exactly what he'd been determined not to do. But as he backed away from Casey's hungry mouth, he realized he had bigger problems on his hands, and then he wondered how he could have been thinking of anything else.

She'd seen his face.

Casey Jones had seen his face.

He blinked at her in the blinding light. Her brown eyes roamed his face as if memorizing every inch of it before they lit with recognition. She remembered him from the hotel.

Without taking her eyes off him, she said, "That's okay, Laura. This is, um, the blind date I was telling you about."

"I figured that out all by myself, sis. It's not like you date so much you'd be seeing two different guys in the same week." She wandered toward the kitchen, and Marcus thought he heard her mutter, "Or in the same year, for that matter."

But he was still staring at Casey. Still shuddering from her kiss. Still feeling as if the bottom had fallen out of his stomach from the lights coming on so suddenly, ending the life he'd lived for more than twenty years. So long he didn't know any other way of life.

"So you're the guy from the pool."

He only nodded, battling the urge to cover his face with his hands or turn away or something. Anything.

"If I'd known, I wouldn't have been so..." Her voice trailed off as she searched his face. "Don't look like that." It was a whisper. Her hand reached out as if to touch his cheek, hesitated, then lowered again.

"Like what?"

"Like my seeing your face is the end of the world as you know it."

He lowered his head, shaking it slowly. "You just don't get it, do you, Casey? It *is*."

"Why?" He didn't answer, but she persisted. "Why Guardian? Because I'm going to rush out to the press with a full description? Or do you think I'll run off posters with your face on them and plaster them all over town?"

He lifted his head slowly. "No one has ever known what the Guardian looks like," he told her.

"So now someone does." She tilted her head to one side, looking every bit as innocent as a woodland fawn. "You can trust me, you know."

He searched her brown eyes and tried to ignore that softening sensation in his heart. Because it was accompanied by panic. He shook it off, that softening. But the panic remained. "No, I don't know that at all."

"Well, you can."

He shrugged, then glanced toward the kitchen when

he heard Laura rattling pots and pans—deliberately, he thought. That particular sort of rattling didn't sound as if it served any other purpose besides making noise.

"What about her?" he asked.

"She doesn't even know your face is a secret in the first place, so why would she go rushing off to describe you to anyone? It's not as if she can spot you in a crowd, nudge the person beside her and say, 'That's him. That's the Guardian.' She doesn't even *know* you're the Guardian. And I'm not going to tell her."

"Aren't you?"

Her eyes were very serious, very deep. "I promise."

He closed his eyes, tilting his head up. She was making it all sound so simple. So easy. But if it was that simple, why did he feel so violated? As if strangers had broken into his solitary hideaway and made themselves at home. Touched his most prized possessions. Ruined his haven.

"Come on, just meet her. You'll feel better once you do."

She got to her feet, tugged on his arm. He sat there, staring down at her hand on his arm, felt the recurrence of the heat sizzling at that tiny point of contact.

"What about...?" He didn't finish.

"That kiss? It's okay to say it, you know."

He met her gaze. "I didn't mean for it to be—"

"So utterly shattering?" she asked, her voice going hoarse. "Especially since you've already made it clear that nothing can happen between us."

"Right."

"It was for my sister's benefit," Casey said slowly. "Don't worry. I understand that it didn't mean a thing. Right?"

"Yeah," he said, watching her face, the way her cheeks colored and she couldn't quite meet his eyes. "Exactly right."

"I never thought otherwise." Her throat moved as if she were trying to swallow and couldn't. Marcus knew that she was lying through her pretty teeth. That kiss had been the farthest thing from "nothing." It had been something. Something to the tenth power.

Something he'd better not let happen again.

He couldn't seem to stop shaking in reaction to a deep-down chill that wouldn't let up. He felt more vulnerable than he ever had in his life. They'd seen his face. And Casey...Casey seemed to see a good deal more than just that. For a man who'd spent his life isolated, unconnected to anyone, it was a lot to deal with all at once.

He was still struggling with this odd feeling of being stripped bare in front of two strangers as Casey coaxed him into the kitchen. Her sister rose from the table, where she'd been sipping a cup of what smelled like hot cocoa, and extended a delicate hand.

"So, do I finally get an introduction?"

"Sure," Casey said, glancing from Marcus to her sister and back again with a nervous little smile. "Go ahead. Introduce yourself."

There was something about the younger woman. She looked haunted—hiding so many secrets in her eyes he couldn't believe she'd be the least bit interested in his.

"Marcus," he muttered, even before he realized he was going to say it. He'd better get on the ball here or they'd have his life story written in his own hand for the asking. He stopped himself before he said any more.

Laura lifted her brows, met his eyes suddenly, then looked away. As if something he'd said or done had bothered her. As if she knew. And she did. She knew all about secrets.

"Laura," she replied, and her smile seemed like a cover. What she was covering he couldn't begin to guess. "You must be something pretty special."

"Must I?"

She nodded. "To have made my sister notice you—yeah, at least. At most, you'd need two heads and a bullhorn."

He grinned at that. Casey was right. He liked this girl. Her hair was just as black as midnight, pulled up in back into a high ponytail that bounced when she moved. And her jet eyes were more than just secretive. They were alive, and warm, and magical.

"Maybe she's just been waiting for the best," he said with a wink, and when Laura laughed, his stomach seemed to puddle inside him like melting chocolate. He didn't like the feeling at all. And he didn't like the way these two women got to him.

"I like this guy," Laura said, and as if to prove it, she turned to reach for another mug and proceeded to make him a cup of cocoa. "Here you go, Mar—" She seemed to stumble over his name, then just skipped it and started over. "Here you go," she said. "I can't judge you thoroughly unless I see how you react to hot cocoa."

He took the cup from her. It felt warm in his hands, the fragrant steam rolling up to his senses. She nodded toward the table, and he sat, shifted in the chair and tried to settle down. This was too cozy. Too damned intimate. He should have left the second the lights had come on. Hell, he should have left long before then.

Instead he sat there, a beautiful woman on each side of him. Both of whom disturbed him in far different ways. Laura had fixed a cup for Casey, as well, so the three of them sat there with their cocoa like some kind of Christmas-card painting.

Then Casey reached over and snapped on the radio, and a seasonal standard filled the room with jingle bells and merry voices. It was all he could take.

He put down his cup and got to his feet. "I have to go."

"Marcus, don't..." Casey got up, too, one hand on his arm.

Laura lowered her head. "Hey, I'm sorry, you two. I didn't mean to break up your evening. I just...I couldn't sleep, and I heard someone down here and I thought..."

Marcus saw the fear before she concealed it once more. "You didn't break anything up—"

"That's not how it looked to me."

"Laura," Casey began with an exasperated glance and a roll of her eyes.

"Laura, I'm not leaving because of you," Marcus said.

"You shouldn't be leaving at all," Laura replied in a rush.

That struck him silent. He sensed there was a real plea behind those words. He blinked and cleared his throat. Told himself not to speak. Not to let the words dancing on the tip of his tongue escape. He even gritted his teeth.

Then he looked into the huge black eyes staring across the table at him, at the fear in Laura's face, and the words gushed out of him like a geyser. "Would you be able to sleep better if I stayed?"

Laura blinked in surprise. "Did I say I couldn't sleep?"

"You sure did."

"Well, did I say why?"

"No. But I can see you're scared, Laura. It's in your eyes."

"Yeah, and I can see you're creative. That's gotta be the best line I've ever heard a guy use to get himself invited to spend the night." She glanced at her sister. "You buying this, Case?"

"Hook, line and sinker," she said. "I vote he stays. How about you?"

"Hey, this is none of my business." But she was looking at Casey as if she didn't know her.

"He'll be sleeping on the sofa," Casey said. "Alone."

"Right."

"Laura!"

"Okay, okay, whatever you say." She slugged

down her cocoa, then eyed Marcus until he took a gulp of his own just to break eye contact.

When he set the cup down she was still looking at him, only now she was smiling. "You have a chocolate mustache." A soft giggle escaped her.

"So do you," he told her, though she didn't. She laughed harder and swiped at her face. And he thought she was an angel. An angel in need of protection. And he was the guy to provide it.

"You can stay," she told him. "Men who drink cocoa neatly are entirely too anal and serious for my sister. She's got enough of that for two, believe me."

"I always thought I was pretty anal and serious," he said, and it was nothing less than the truth.

"Then it must be the company," Laura confessed.

"Must be."

There was something going on between this girl and him. That it was obvious didn't become apparent until Casey cleared her throat rather uncomfortably, and Marcus broke eye contact with Laura, looked at Casey and felt himself battle an urge to explain. And then he wasn't sure he could if he wanted to. He felt something for Laura. But it was different—totally different from the feelings he had swirling around inside him for Casey. And none of it mattered, because he didn't intend to let himself continue feeling at all. Nothing. Not for *either* of the Jones women.

He was insane to be staying here. Totally insane.

She must be out of her mind. Casey yanked cushions from the sofa bed and hurled them carelessly onto the floor, then bent to haul the mattress out of its hiding place. What the hell had come over her in the past two hours? Who was this lunatic running around in her body, anyway? It sure as hell wasn't Casey Jones, intrepid reporter, revealer of secrets, independent woman no more in need of a man than of a second head. Because she'd practically stood on her head to get him in here. And then she'd flirted with him. She'd come on to him so shamelessly she might as well have just come right out and told him she'd really like to jump his bones.

She pushed a hand backward through her hair and wondered what the hell had come over her. Marcus—*if* that was his real name—and Laura were still in the kitchen sipping cocoa. And come to think of it, that wasn't *her* real name, either. No wonder those two hit it off so well. Laura looking at Marcus with her big dark eyes. Marcus staring back at her, as stunned as if Cupid's arrow had just nailed him right in the backside. Casey sitting there feeling like chopped liver.

Casey swallowed that selfish feeling. Or tried to. True, she hadn't been this attracted to a man in…in her life. But if Laura liked him, then…

Oh hell, why did Laura have to like him?

She crammed a pillow into a clean case as if she were stuffing a sausage and flung it into the chair beside the sofa bed. Then she snapped a fitted sheet onto one corner of the mattress.

Then she sighed. At least one good thing had come of all this. She'd seen his face. She was the one and only reporter in the entire universe to have done so. She knew the true identity of the Guardian.

Well, maybe not his whole identity. She knew his face, though.

Yeah. She knew his face. Sighing, she let go of the sheet, smoothed a hand over it and sat down slowly on the bed. He had a great face, not a pretty one. Not a soft one. But square and boxy, rugged in its harsh lines and angles. Bronzed skin despite his life in the darkness. He must see the sun sometime, she mused, or else he had a tanning bed somewhere that got a lot of use. His eyes were a matched pair of shiny black olives. In color, a lot like Laura's eyes, but the shape differed. Hers were round, wide and innocent. His, narrow and wary, almond-shaped and tilting upward. So much suspicion lurked in their ebony depths it seemed it would spill out and poison everyone around him. So much distrust. A dark wall lined those eyes, a wall designed to keep people out. And she wondered if those eyes ever softened. If anyone had ever seen them smile or warm with feeling.

He didn't seem to display much of that. Feeling. He had feelings, though, but kept them prisoner—life sentence in solitary.

His dark hair was cut short and neat, yet she doubted that matched his personality. The style seemed conservative and respectable. But he seemed like a caged lion, a wild man waiting to be cut loose. A frustrated man who didn't even know that he was hiding behind a facade of heroism.

He stepped in from the kitchen. His footsteps didn't alert her to his presence until after his aura did. She sensed him before she heard him.

She only stiffened for a moment. Quickly she resumed her task, smoothing the top sheet over the fitted one, folding the corners.

"I'd have done that myself."

"Don't be silly. I don't mind at all."

"Sure you do." He came closer, reached around her and took the folded corner from her hands. "I'm not used to being waited on by a woman, Casey."

"I'm not used to having overnight houseguests," she countered.

"So I gathered from what your sister said."

Casey closed her eyes. "She talks too much." Casey gently moved his arms aside so she could step away from him, put some distance between them. "But she's a wonderful person, Marcus. And I'm not going to let her get hurt."

He sighed, lowered his head. "Neither am I." Turning slowly, Marcus paced away from her, then stopped and faced her once more. "I know it's awkward...my spending the night. I didn't mean to offer, it just sort of...came out."

"Laura can have that effect on men sometimes."

He frowned, tilted his head to one side. "It's just that she seemed so frightened—"

Casey held up one hand like a traffic cop. "Hey, no need to explain anything to me. I'm the one who talked you into coming in here in the first place, right?" Something was showing in her eyes, she could tell by the way he was searching them, so she looked away.

"You think I'm interested in her, don't you, Casey?"

Casey only shook her head and started forward,

moving past Marcus and toward the stairs. "It's none of my business who you're interested in, Marcus. I could care less—"

He grabbed her arm when she moved past him, his grip firm but not painful. "You're a liar."

"Let go of me, Marcus."

"Not until I make something very clear to you, Casey. Look at me." She didn't, so he said it again. "Look at me."

Slowly she moved her gaze upward until it locked with his.

"Now, listen carefully, because I'm only going to explain this to you once. I don't do relationships, Casey. I don't do dates or flowers or promises. I don't fall in love, don't even believe in it. Do you understand all that?"

"Perfectly," she whispered, her heart in her throat. "I got the message, 'Guardian.'"

"No, I don't think you did. Not yet. I don't want your sister, Casey. I want you."

Her heart stopped. Her eyes widened. "B-but you just said..."

"I know what I said. I said it for a reason. It's fair, don't you think, that I tell you up front? So that when it happens, you'll know the rules."

She felt her temper rising like a flame into her face. "The *rules?*"

He nodded and slowly released her arm.

She lifted a hand and gripped his instead. "So you don't feel a thing for me, but you're still willing to have sex."

He looked a bit guilty. "It's what we both want. You've made that pretty obvious, Casey."

"Sex without feeling? That's what I want?"

He shook his head, started to turn away.

"Just a minute, Marcus. I have a few *rules* of my own to tell you about."

One brow rose higher than the other as he faced her again. "Do you?"

She ignored the flutter in her stomach and rushed on. "Yeah. Rule number one—no casual sex. No flings. No one-night stands. No sex of any kind with men who don't believe in *love*. Sorry, Marcus, but the farthest you're going to get with me will be in your dreams tonight."

He gaped at her. Then he shrugged. "I think you're wrong, but I'm not going to argue about it."

"That's good, because it's an argument you'd lose." She bent to the bottom step, picked up the folded comforter and threw it at him. "There's your blanket. Good night."

"Sweet dreams."

"You just better sleep lightly. If anything happens tonight—"

"Your sister will be perfectly safe tonight, Casey." He rolled his eyes. "So will you."

"Why am I not reassured?"

He shrugged. "Oh, you know I'll protect you from the bad guys. You're just wondering who's going to protect you from me."

"I think I can manage that part fine all by myself," she said.

"We'll see." He lifted his hands to the front of his shirt and began to unbutton it.

A flash of skin was all it took to remind Casey how he'd looked in the hotel hot tub. Hard, lean muscle and tanned flesh. She remembered his arms around her in the water, the way they'd felt. The way she'd felt.

She tore her gaze away from his chest and headed up the stairs. But she didn't really think she'd sleep.

Her prediction proved accurate. She tossed and turned and tried to still her ridiculous, illogical mind. Odd, since her mind wasn't normally illogical at all.

Would Laura be upset? Had she really been attracted to him? It didn't matter. She would change her mind when she found out what a slug he was. No relationships—just sex—was basically what he'd told Casey. What a jerk.

But he wanted her, not her sister.

She caught herself smiling, then stopped.

Well, so much for any silly romantic notion that might have made its way into her brain for even the slightest moment. He was here to do a job, period. Protect Laura until Casey could get to the bottom of what was going on with her. After that he could go back to his life of crime fighting. But he wouldn't forget her. Not ever.

Because she was the only person in the world who knew who he was. And it put her that much closer to discovering the story behind the man.

Seven

When in a state of panic, come on like a total idiot.

It wasn't an axiom Marcus had heard anywhere, so he figured he must have made it up himself.

Casey Jones scared the hell out of him. So did her sister. And he didn't even know why. He'd faced down armed killers with less trepidation.

The two femmes fatales had gone up to their respective beds. He didn't know if they were sleeping, but if the circles around the younger one's eyes were anything to go by, she at least was probably awake.

Her man-killer of an older sister was probably sound asleep and utterly peaceful. She certainly wasn't lying awake staring at the ceiling and wishing she could relive the past twenty-four hours. Like he was.

Hell, he wouldn't know what to do differently, anyway. Except get the hell out of this house before Laura turned the spotlight on him. Human relationships were one skill he hadn't mastered at the feet of his mentor. Caine had been every bit as solitary as Marcus was. And probably just as clueless in... certain areas.

And the part about lying awake all night was irrelevant. He couldn't go to sleep on the job—had been trained far too well for that. The thing was, he couldn't have slept even if he'd wanted to with his mind all stirred up and boiling over.

What was it about the two women that put him in such a state?

He sat on the sofa bed, wide-awake, and tried to quiet his mind. Deep breathing. Meditation. But not too deep. He needed to be aware of everything going on around him. Every sound, every movement. Every presence.

And he needed to forget about the ladies upstairs. Especially Casey.

"So just how serious is this thing, Casey?"

Casey curled her legs underneath her on the foot of Laura's bed. She'd only come in to check on her sister, but Laura had been awake, waiting and determined to make conversation.

"Not serious at all, sis."

"Really?" Laura's eyes opened wide, her brows arching in surprise. "Gee, I never knew you kissed men that way if you weren't at least mildly serious about them."

"Well, you never walked in on my dates before."

"Not that there have been many to walk in on."

"Maybe I don't tell you everything, little sister."

Laura shook her head. "Yes, you do. You've always been an open book. That's why I'm trying hard to ignore this feeling that Marcus down there is more than just a boyfriend."

"Try less. Way less. He's an acquaintance."

"So you wouldn't mind if I asked him out myself?"

Casey's head came up so fast she wrenched her neck.

Laura smiled broadly. "I knew it!" she exploded, slapping both hands on the covers.

"Knew what? You're welcome to him, Laura, but I'd better warn you in advance—he doesn't 'do relationships.' Just one-night stands."

"That's ridiculous," Laura said.

"It's what he said."

"He's a man. What does he know?"

Casey lowered her head with a sigh she didn't mean to emit, and Laura crawled lower on the bed and touched her shoulders. "Hey, you know I was only trying to get a rise out of you, right? I don't have any interest in your Marcus."

"Really? 'Cause, Laura, if you do, I'll step aside. I could never let any man come between us."

Laura smiled gently. "I love you for that. Because I know this guy means a lot more to you than you're letting on, Case. But no, I'm being honest here. I mean…I like him. I liked him right off the bat. He's got a way about him…almost makes me feel as if I know him already, like a dear old friend or something." She shrugged. "Or maybe it's just because of his name that I felt instantly close to him."

"His name?" Casey narrowed her eyes. "What about his name?"

Laura's gaze became shuttered. "Never mind. What I'm trying to get across here is that I think Marcus and I could be very good friends. Family even, if…well, you know, if this thing goes that far. But I don't feel even a twinge of anything romantic where he's concerned.''

Casey shrugged as if it didn't matter. ''Well, maybe I don't, either.''

''Yeah, and maybe you don't believe in freedom of the press. But I doubt it.''

Casey snatched a pillow from the foot of the bed and threw it at her sister. Laura caught it, laughing. ''Go to bed, Casey. Or go back downstairs and convince that man he most definitely *does* do relationships.''

Casey made a face but got to her feet. ''You sure you're going to be able to sleep, Laura?''

''Sure. Go on.''

Casey nodded but knew her sister was lying through her teeth. ''I'll be right next door if you need me, kiddo.''

''Oh. Well, it's his loss.''

''Just bang on the wall if you get antsy.''

''Will do. 'Night, Case.''

'''Night.'' Casey left her sister's room, closed the door behind her and stood in the hallway for a long moment.

Not a sound came up from downstairs. Was Marcus sound asleep already? And how the heck did he intend to keep Laura safe if he was sleeping?

She battled between her pride telling her not to be so interested in what he was doing and her curiosity. As it had all her life, her curiosity won. She tiptoed along the hall, paused at the top of the stairs and peered down.

All the lights were off, and the sofa's back was to her. She couldn't see him at all. Silently she padded down the steps. One by one, lower and lower. She stood in the living room now, in the utter darkness, and waited a minute, listening for his breathing. But she heard nothing. It was as if he'd disappeared.

Had he? Had he run out on her? Abandoned Laura just because of a simple disagreement?

All right, not so simple, but…

Casey stepped forward. A floorboard creaked and she froze, grimacing. Shooting a glance toward the sofa bed, she waited for some reaction, but none came. So she stepped again, thanking her stars when the floor kept quiet this time. And again, still farther, until she stood right beside the bed. But all she saw when she blinked through the darkness were some rumpled covers and a pillow bearing the indentation where his head had rested.

Then someone grabbed her from behind, spun her around so fast she almost tipped over and flung her backward onto the bed. Before she had time to cry out, he was on top of her, straddling her, with his big hand clapped tight over her mouth.

Blinking in absolute terror, she willed her vision to clear and finally stared up at him. Marcus. The Guardian. Great. So if they happened to be attacked tonight by a five-foot-two-inch, hundred-and-ten-pound reporter, he'd be able to handle it just fine.

Recognition dawned in his dark eyes. But instead of getting up, he stayed where he was. "What are you doing down here?"

"Mmf-mmf," she replied.

"Again, please?" he said, removing his hand from her mouth.

She glared at him. "Oh hell, Marcus, what do you *think* I'm doing down here? Checking to see if you snore for the exposé I'm writing?"

He only kept studying her with those dark eyes.

"It was quiet," she said, wishing he'd move. It felt too tempting having him stay where he was. "I was afraid you might have left."

"I wouldn't leave, Casey. And I think you know it."

She shrugged. "I wanted to make sure."

"Are you sure that's all you wanted?"

"Get off me, you big lug."

He stared down at her a second longer. Then he got up slowly, turning as he did, so he wound up sitting beside her on the edge of the sofa bed. He didn't look at her. Instead he lowered his head and blew a sigh that sounded frustrated to her. "Sorry," he finally said. "I'm trained to react. I hear someone sneaking around, I pounce on them."

"I'll keep that in mind."

"It would be a good idea."

Headlights came through the window, casting lively shadows on the walls, on the rumpled bed, on Marcus's unclothed chest, and then the light faded as the vehicle passed.

It was almost erotic.

Until he sent a worried glance after the car.

"What is it?"

"Maybe nothing. But that's the third time that vehicle has passed by tonight."

Casey blinked, glanced toward the window, the closed curtains, and back at him again. He hadn't moved. "You couldn't have seen that car from here."

"No. The sound of the engine is enough. It bugs me, the way the driver eases up on the accelerator as he passes the house. There's no sharp curve out there. No reason for it."

A dryness coated Casey's throat and she couldn't swallow. "You think it's the same person who's stalking my sister?"

"You have anyone else with a reason to case this place on a regular basis? Maybe the police checking on things?"

She shook her head. "But what do they want? They already know we live here, they broke in once."

"What they want is to make sure you're alone. And home. And that it's you in here and not some decoys or cops. Not some kind of a trap."

She drew a shuddering breath. "Hell, I should never have brought Laura back here."

"No. You were right to bring her back. I can't catch these guys unless they make another move on her."

Casey whirled on him, wide-eyed. "No, Marcus, that's not what I want! God, I never intended to use my sister as bait. I only wanted you to protect her until I could get to the bottom of all of this. I won't put her at risk—"

"Casey." He put his hands on her shoulders, silencing her instantly. And then he held her eyes while he spoke. "Laura is perfectly safe as long as I'm here.

And what better way to get to the bottom of this than to catch the bastards and make them tell us? Hmm?''

She blinked, trying to sort out the chaos in her mind. "But what if they get past us? What if something happens—"

"No one gets past me. Didn't I just prove that?"

There was a teasing light in his eyes, one that made her heart trip and assured her he was telling her nothing less than the truth.

"I'm scared, Marcus."

"I know."

"You don't know how much I love her. How much she means to me. What it would do to me if I lost her." With a shudder, she lowered her head to hide her tears.

"Yes," he said. "I do."

She brushed the tears from her eyes. "I'm sorry. I know you do, Marcus. I shouldn't have said that."

"It doesn't matter," he told her, his voice gruff, his back to her now. "Not anymore. All that matters is that you understand. I know what's at stake here. And I'm not going to let anything happen to Laura. This is one little sister the bastards of the world aren't going to touch."

So much emotion in his voice. As if his heart were pounding inside every word. And she couldn't help herself. She moved closer to him, slipped her arms around his waist and lowered her head to rest against his back. "I'm sorry, Marcus. You must miss her so much."

He cleared his throat, but it sounded ineffective.

"Laura…reminds me of her. In some odd, ridiculous way."

"So that's what it is."

He nodded. "That's what it is." Stiffening his back, he covered her hands with his own and gently moved them away from his waist. "And that's *all* it is."

"Not that you need to tell me that," she whispered as he turned to face her once more. "It doesn't matter, does it? I mean, since you don't believe in relationships…or love."

She could see the torment in his eyes. "Maybe it's more that I can't."

"Why, Marcus?"

His eyes glistened. Shiny dark marbles in the night. Roaming her face so intensely she could almost feel their touch. "I couldn't go through it again."

"The loss, you mean?"

He nodded. "It wasn't just Sara. It was all of them. All of them…." He clamped his jaw shut, turned away, headed for the door.

"Marcus, wait."

But he didn't wait. He gripped the doorknob and pulled it open in one swift, jerky motion. "I'll be outside. You'll be safe. Don't worry."

"But—"

"I have to get out of here, Casey. I can't seem to shut the hell up around you. You're drawing things out of me that I've never told anyone, and it's dangerous, dammit!"

He stepped out into the night, then stopped, hand still gripping the doorknob. For a moment, she thought he'd turn around, face her again, apologize for raising his voice. But he didn't. He simply sighed heavily, chin dropping toward his chest, and pulled the door shut behind him.

And that was all.

And she wanted him more than she ever had.

He stayed outside. Safe. Protected by the night, the darkness, his beloved cloak. He liked the cold, because it was like solitude. No warmth could keep him this sharp, this acute. No sunshine could make his vision any clearer, his mind any more alert.

No woman could fulfill him the way his life as the Guardian did. Never.

When daylight broke he watched the house a little more relaxed, but just as alert. It was unlikely anyone would make a move by day. Any pro, at least. And he had the feeling that's what they were dealing with here. A pro.

So he watched, more for himself than from any sense of impending danger. He saw Casey moving around inside, her shadow falling across the closed curtains, rippling over the fabric. He watched the peculiar morning rituals of those two shadow women. The identical way they had of bending over, flipping their heads upside down so their hair hung toward the floor while they wielded a hair dryer in one hand and a brush in the other. First Laura performed this interesting ritual while Casey vanished into the bathroom, and then Casey repeated it.

It made Marcus smile to see. Some sisterly traits,

he mused, must not be genetic. Hair flipping being one of them.

He found himself smiling and caught his lower lip between his teeth. Damn, he was doing that entirely too much when he thought of those two.

He waited, though every instinct was telling him to run, and only left after the two ladies did, both in the same car, with Casey driving. The blue Mustang he'd admired. He knew the routine. Casey would drop Laura off at the elementary school and then head over to her job in the city. A women's-wear boutique on Main Street. Right next to the offices of the local gossip sheet known as *Lone Star*. He didn't suppose the magazine was quite as despicable as *Prominence Magazine*, the one that had plastered his name and alleged likeness all over the country, but Marcus figured they were all pretty much alike. They'd print whatever they thought might sell more issues, and morals didn't happen to enter into it. The people who worked for that kind of publication didn't have an honest bone in their bodies. None of them. They must teach Ethical Bankruptcy in Journalism 101.

He made his way to the car, followed a safe distance behind Casey's Mustang until she dropped her sister off at the school. Then he watched until Laura got safely inside.

Casey had assured him the school was a safe place for her sister. Hesitant to take her word for it, he'd checked the place out himself and found she'd been right. No attempt would be made on Laura while she was at work. A pro would attack where she was most vulnerable, and any pro could see that was at home.

Especially one who didn't know the Guardian was lurking in the shadows.

Laura entered the school building safely, nodding to the security men at the doors as she passed. Men who, Casey assured him, had been tipped off about Laura's situation and who would be discreet about it, while keeping an extra eye on her.

Satisfied Laura was safe for the day, Marcus turned around and headed back to the hotel. He needed to get some sleep before going back on duty. Graham would be manning the computer by now. If anything happened to Casey or Laura, the magic of Graham's network would let him know it, and he could be there within minutes.

Meanwhile, he was exhausted.

When he dragged himself out of the private elevator to the penthouse suite, he was so looking forward to falling into a big soft bed that he'd even stopped trying to analyze his confused feelings for the two women. But when he stepped into the suite, Graham was there waiting, file folder in hand, and a hesitant look in his eyes.

"What's this?" Marcus stepped the rest of the way in and closed the door.

Graham came closer, taking Marcus's long dark coat and his fedora, before placing the manila folder in his hands. "I'm afraid you're not going to like it, Marcus."

"Then why not wait until after I have a much needed nap to show it to me?" He was only half-kidding.

"I'm afraid it's something you would prefer to

know about right away. Actually, you might have pre-ferred to have known about it yesterday, but without the computer I had no way of—"

"I hope you're not apologizing, Graham. You're a wizard, and if something slipped by you, that only proves to me that no one on the planet would have caught it, myself included."

"Yes, well..." Graham turned away, and Marcus thought he was probably touched by the compliment. "You might change your mind about that when you read what I've learned this morning."

Sighing, Marcus flipped open the folder and fanned through sheets and sheets of printouts. Then he closed the file again, dropping it on the coffee table as he headed for the easy chair. He sank into the chair, leaned back, closed his eyes.

"Any chance you could give me the condensed version, old friend?"

"Of course. Perhaps you'd like a drink first?"

Marcus's eyes shot open. "That bad, is it?"

"I'm afraid so."

"Then you'd better give it to me straight."

Assuming he was referring to the whiskey rather than the news, Graham quickly poured a double, handed it to him and paced away. "Your Casey Jones hasn't been entirely honest with you, Marcus. And I have to say, I'm very sorry to have to tell you about it."

Marcus came to attention. He sat up straighter in his chair, tossed back the drink and set the glass down hard. "She's been lying to me?"

"Withholding the truth."

"Is there a difference?"

"There could be a very large difference, Marcus. And I'd advise you to find out for sure why she chose not to tell you this before you—"

"What didn't she tell me, Graham?"

Graham's throat moved convulsively, then he said, "She's a reporter for a magazine called *Lone Star*."

"What!" Marcus came out of the chair so fast he knocked the empty tumbler from the table to the floor. Damn thing didn't even have the decency to shatter. It bounced, hit him in the shin and then rolled under his chair.

"I'm afraid it's true."

He just stood there, gaping, not believing it. Then he snatched the file folder off the table and flipped through it, frenzied for details. For proof. It couldn't be true. Not Casey. She wouldn't—

But it was all there, and while he didn't feel the least bit like sleeping anymore, he did feel tired. More tired than he'd felt in a long time.

"Her specialty seems to be exposés, as you can see from the tear sheets I was able to download."

"I can see that."

"So you understand why I felt you should be warned right away. I was afraid—"

"Afraid I might be the subject of her next column."

"It would explain a lot," Graham said. "The problem is, I could find no evidence she'd lied about anything else. Everything she told you about her sister, the adoption and the secrecy surrounding it is utterly true. And her home was broken into. The police report confirms—"

"All the police report confirms is that she called them and told them someone had broken in. A woman as clever as Casey Jones could easily have set the whole thing up herself."

"Then...then you think all of this has been a scam designed to expose you?"

"If it is, we should know soon enough."

Graham frowned. Then his brows shot up and his eyes widened. "You didn't tell her—"

"No. But she saw my face, Graham. She knows enough to destroy me."

"Oh, no." Graham lowered his head, pinching the bridge of his nose between thumb and forefinger while shaking his head.

Marcus paced and felt like rubbing his own forehead. "Dammit, I can't believe she fooled me so easily." Then he paused, turning slowly. "Yet even knowing this, I could swear that Laura's fear is real. She isn't faking it."

"Unless she's an accomplished actress. As talented as her sister, perhaps."

"Nobody's as talented as Casey," Marcus said. "I could kill her for this. I could put my hands around her throat and—"

"Then I suggest you stay away from her until the feeling passes." When Marcus reached for the bottle, Graham snatched it out of reach, filled his glass but didn't surrender the bottle. "And I might also suggest one more drink be your limit, Marcus. You'll want to be stone sober when you confront her."

"You're damned right I will. I want to see those brown eyes when I tell her I know the truth."

Graham blinked but said nothing, though his surprise was plain in his eyes, along with his real concern. Marcus understood it and wished he'd clamped down on his venom. Sure, he should be angry, but not furious, not as enraged as he was right now. It must be obvious to Graham that he'd let things go too far with Casey. Maybe not physically—but in a lot of ways this was worse. She'd invaded his emotions, dug herself into his mind, his thoughts. She'd drawn his private pain out of him like a magnet, reached past his defenses without even working up a sweat. And she'd seen his face.

What the hell was he going to do about that now?

Marcus was lying when he said he didn't believe in love. In relationships. In sharing. Because Casey sensed that he did. Maybe Laura was right and he just didn't realize it.

Oh, sure, he came on all independent and arrogant and macho. But he'd revealed himself to her. People usually did once she set her mind to getting under their skin—although she'd never wanted to get under anybody's skin the way she wanted to get under his.

He'd been hurt. His poor heart had been torn to shreds when he lost his sister—Sara, he'd called her. And there had been more than that. "Not just Sara, all of them. All of them." The catch in his voice when he'd said it had nearly brought her to tears. All of them. Sara and his parents. When, where? Did it matter? Not to Casey.

It didn't take a psychology degree to tell her that experience had shaped him into the man he was today. He'd loved and lost in what had to have been a horrible, heartbreaking and traumatic way. No wonder he didn't want to risk caring again.

Oh, hell. She had no choice now. She *had* to find out all about him. About his past, his life now, this old pain that was still eating away at him.

Casey was born a snoop. That trait was a good one, the way she saw it. It was one she'd parlayed into a successful career. Her other most prominent character trait was one that was a little less desirable. She tended toward nurturing. She'd never been one to bring home wounded birds and mend their wings. Instead she'd brought home troubled classmates. From day one she'd seen herself as the fixer of all life's problems. The protector of the weak, the champion of the frightened. If a boy was threatened by the town bully, she'd be the one to gather every kid in the class together and cajole them into walking the threatened kid home. And she'd make them keep doing it, too, until the bully backed down.

It was probably why she'd taken to Laura from the start. The sense that her new little sister needed protecting. Maybe it was a character flaw. Maybe it made her feel stronger and more powerful if she could fix other people's lives for them. Or maybe it kept her from focusing on her own life and all the things it lacked. She wasn't sure.

She only knew that while she'd been attracted—powerfully attracted—to Marcus before, now she was obsessed. She wanted to know everything about him.

She wanted him to open up to her, to trust her, to let her in so she could wield her magic wand and heal him.

Unless…unless he didn't *want* to be healed.

Oh hell, that was just silly. Of course he wanted to be healed. No one wanted to go around hurting all the time.

Once again, Casey spent her lunch hour digging into the past of the most secretive man she'd ever met. The most secretive *person* she'd ever met.

Besides one. Her own sister, Laura.

Eight

He was waiting when she came home that night.

Casey knew he would be. She'd been running late all afternoon, and Laura had insisted they stop for a few groceries on the way home. So it was dark when they finally pulled in the driveway at 8:00 p.m. But he was there. She could feel his presence the moment she got out of the car.

She was nervous. Jittery as a teenager on a first date. Eager to see him again, half-afraid she'd been wrong about the wounded heart she'd glimpsed inside him last night. What if he laughed at her? What if he really was as cold and unapproachable as he tried to make everyone believe?

No. He wasn't. He was hurting. She could make it better. If she could just get him to open up, she could...

"Casey? You coming?"

She turned to see her sister, a grocery bag in each arm, standing at the front door. "Sorry, Laura. I was thinking." Casey hurried to snatch the remaining bag from the car, then trotted up the front steps to reach past Laura and unlock the door.

"Thinking, huh? About who?"

"No one."

Laura sent her a knowing grin and carried her groceries inside to set them on the table. "Liar."

Casey ignored her, set her bag down and went to peer outside the window.

"Hey, unless the guy's got the place under surveillance, Casey, he can't possibly know you're home yet. Give him a few minutes, will you?"

Casey dropped the curtain and turned. "You're making a lot more out of this than there is, you know."

"Am I really?" Laura shrugged. "Somehow I doubt it." She tugged at her blouse. "But I'll tease you later. Right now I need a shower."

"Go ahead. I'll put the groceries away."

Laura didn't argue. She just smiled and hurried upstairs. Before she'd been gone five minutes, there was a tap at the back door, and Casey glanced up to see Marcus standing on the other side. He looked...dark. She shivered and opened the door.

"We need to talk." He said it without preamble, stepping into the kitchen, closing the door behind him.

She took a step back when he came closer. The reaction was automatic, an instinctive response to the anger emanating from him. "What—what's wrong? You're upset about something."

"No kidding." He took another step toward her.

She took another step back. "Well, are you going to tell me what?"

"Why don't you tell me, Casey? What could I have

found out about you that would make me this angry? That you'd lied to me, maybe?''

She swallowed hard. "About…what?"

"Have there been so many lies you can't be sure?"

Blinking fast, she lowered her gaze, feeling ashamed, though she shouldn't. She had no reason to. She'd done nothing wrong. "No. No, Marcus, there's only been one lie. And I knew you'd find out eventually. I just…"

"Just thought you'd get all you could on me before I did. You going for the front page, Casey? Big byline? Syndication?"

Lifting her chin a notch, she met his eyes again. "I'm not writing any article about you, Marcus."

"Aren't you?"

She held his gaze, willing him to believe her while battling the disappointment that rinsed through her. She supposed she'd let her expectations get too high. She'd been so looking forward to seeing him again— only to have him arrive angry and spouting accusations. She felt like crying.

"Listen to me—"

"No, you listen to me. I don't work with reporters.''

"That's why I didn't tell you I was one. And that's the only reason. Marcus, I knew you'd refuse to protect Laura if you knew—"

"And I don't work with liars."

She flinched. His words stung. Then the anger came. She felt its heat suffuse her face, but her voice remained level and low, only trembling slightly. "You do now."

His eyes went narrow. "Be careful, Casey. That sounds like a threat."

Casey lowered her head. "I hate this. You don't know me well enough to know that about me, I suppose, but I do. I hate deception of any kind, and I never lie. But there's nothing I wouldn't do for my sister, Marcus. Nothing. That's why I went to all that trouble to get in touch with you, why I kept the truth about my career from you and why I'm going to resort to the most despicable tactics I can think of right now. For her, Marcus. Because I love her, and I'm afraid her life is in danger."

Marcus, when she dared to meet his gaze again, was probing her with his eyes, scanning her face as if trying to see inside her brain. "What despicable tactics are you referring to, Casey? Blackmail?"

"If that's what it takes. I know what you look like. I can see that face of yours every time I close my eyes, even if I don't particularly want to." She bit her lip and heard him catch his breath as he turned away. "I could have a composite artist draw a sketch of you so lifelike it would fool your own mother. And I know your first name. I could make a lot of money, earn myself a pile of recognition with the article I could write about you, Marcus. But I never planned to. And I won't...unless you force me."

She chanced a peek at him, but his face was so frightening in its fury that she couldn't look for long.

"I believe you will," he said. "The problem is, Casey, I believe it's what you planned all along. In fact I'm beginning to doubt any of what you told me about your sister is even true. You probably staged the whole—"

He broke off then as Laura came skipping down the stairs in an oversize pink terry robe with a towel wrapped turban-style around her head. She smiled her hello at Marcus. Marcus nodded back. "Glad you finally got here," Laura said. "Casey was burning holes through the window glass watching for you."

She traipsed straight through to the kitchen. "Hey, I thought you were going to put this stuff away," she called. "Never mind. Maybe I'll find a snack in one of these…"

Casey kept her voice to a strangled whisper. "You're very wrong about me, Marcus. I never intended any of this. All I wanted was some help protecting my sister."

"Why don't I believe that?"

"Because you're a bitter, skeptical man who paints every journalist with the same brush. And because…I think you're more comfortable not believing me. I think you're scared to death of the alternative."

He rolled his eyes but looked away. "You don't know as much about me as you think you do. There is no alternative, as you so quaintly put it. There never was. For you it was part of the act. For me, a pleasant diversion. Period."

"Now who's the liar?"

He shot her a killing glance.

"Will you protect my sister, Marcus? Or will I write that article?"

"Your sister never needed protecting. When are you going to drop the act and admit that?"

He took a step forward, reaching out to grip her wrists as he spoke.

And then, from the kitchen, Laura screamed.

Marcus was looking at Casey when that sound ripped through him. There was no mistaking the panic in her face. The skin went white, instantly white. Her eyes widened and her body went rigid. He had an instant to realize his own reaction was different. He felt sick inside. He'd turned off the sensor when he'd come in, and he'd been so immersed in his own misery, he'd forgotten to turn it back on. Laura's scream brought an old memory to life. The distant echo of that other scream, the one that still haunted him at night. The final scream of his mother. The name she had shrieked—the one that still eluded him.

All of that rushed through his mind in the space of a heartbeat. And then he was moving, letting instinct take over. Part of him knew Casey was right behind him. But most of him was focused on what he saw in the kitchen when he burst into the room. Laura's legs and feet, twisting and kicking as she was pulled out the back door and into the darkness. The way she tried to grip the door frame with one foot as the man dragged her through. The way her slipper fell to the floor.

Marcus assessed it all very quickly. He could see the man outside, in the darkness. A big man, totally bald so the top of his head gleamed with the light's reflection. Dressed in black. No weapons visible. Both hands busy restraining his struggling victim. One hand over her mouth, so the only sounds she could make were muffled grunts and moans. His gaze on her instead of on what was happening in the house. Sloppy. Very sloppy.

Silently, Marcus backed into the living room, reaching behind him to press a finger to Casey's lips when she drew a breath to protest. Out of the attacker's sight, he turned to face her. "Lock the doors, turn out the lights and get yourself out of sight. Then call 911."

"I already tried. The phone lines are out."

He nodded, having expected as much. "Go on, get out of sight."

She bit her lip, tears welling in her eyes as she nodded. Marcus had to trust her to do as he said. There was no time not to. He whirled and headed out the front door, then forced himself to slow his pace. Back against the side of the house, keeping to the shadows—it came so naturally he barely had to think about what he was doing. He slipped into the narrow grassy alley between house and garage, moving swiftly without a sound, his feet rolling over the lush lawn in smooth steps that barely disturbed the greenery.

He emerged into the back lawn only a few seconds from the time the thug had dragged Laura outside. A guy the size of Laura's attacker wouldn't move very fast. Marcus peered around the corner of the house.

The large man was still struggling with Laura, only a few yards from the door, and his back was to Marcus. Perfect. Marcus moved forward, soundlessly, and then he struck. The kidney punch was enough to get the jerk's attention. He whirled defensively, swinging those beefy fists as he did, but by then Marcus was moving again. He hit the ground, somersaulted and sprung to his feet in a new position, then punched the attacker in the face.

Blood spattered, seemingly propelled by the loud grunt the man emitted. He swung at Marcus again, but Marcus caught his arm this time, turning, bending slightly, then straightening fast. The man flew over Marcus's back to land several feet away on the ground.

Marcus heard Casey's voice behind him as she raced out the back door. "Come on, Laura. Get up, get inside. God, are you all right?"

He turned toward the sound of that voice, distracted when he knew better than to let himself be. Laura huddled on the ground, shaking like a wet leaf, while her sister urged her to her feet, tugging, talking, pulling.

Damn the woman, he'd told her to stay inside.

Running footsteps alerted him to his mistake, and he spun again, only to see his mark making a fast break across the back lawn.

"Go!" Casey shouted. "Go after him, dammit!"

But Marcus stood where he was, every sense heightened. "And leave you two here for his partner?"

The man vanished from sight, and then there was the slam of a car door, the sound of an engine roaring to life and tires spitting gravel.

"You...you think there's another one?"

Marcus scanned the darkness as far as he could see, probed the shadows with his sharp eyes, listened, *felt* for a second presence. Then he sighed and went back to the two women. Laura, standing now, was wrapped in Casey's arms, her entire body shaking violently, her dark hair sticking to her tearstained face. Eyes as wide as the moon. He moved closer, pushed some of her hair out of her eyes. Laura stepped out of her sister's arms, but her stance didn't look too solid. She'd fall if she didn't sit down soon.

"No. I don't think so. But there could have been, and I couldn't take the risk. Besides, he had a car waiting nearby. I'd never have caught him."

Laura closed her eyes. "Th-thank you, Marcus. He—he would have…" A sob choked her, and the next thing Marcus knew, she was in *his* arms. Her small head on his shoulder, tears wetting his shirt. Something welled up in his heart. A memory. Sara, crying in his arms just like this. He was nine and she was just three, and her kitten had disappeared. It was as if her world had ended. And though he'd secretly thought it incredibly stupid and childish to sob like that over a cat, he'd held her. He'd told her he would make it okay, and she'd believed him. The next day he'd drafted an army of his school chums and they'd turned the neighborhood upside down despite the pouring rain. And they'd found the dumb kitten, lost in a vacant lot nearby. He'd never forget Sara's eyes when he'd brought that mongrel home to her. It looked like a drowned rat, but you'd have thought he'd given her a diamond. She glowed. Her eyes just sparkled and her smile…

That was the first time he'd felt like anybody's hero.

Marcus had to squeeze his eyes tight against the burning moisture gathering there. It was one of the many memories that had been lost to him for the past twenty-odd years. But now it was back. And he wasn't sure whether to be grateful or sorry, because it hurt so damn much.

He closed his arms around Laura when he felt her weakening, and he met Casey's tear-filled eyes. "Let's get you inside," he said, fully aware his voice was gruff. He scooped Laura up and nodded at Casey, who went ahead to open the door for them. As he carried Laura inside, Casey remained close beside him, stroking her sister's face, speaking softly to her, trying to keep her own terror in check.

She led the way upstairs to Laura's bedroom, and Marcus laid the young woman on her bed and took a step back. It was disturbing to hold her. It brought back things—things he'd rather leave buried in his forgotten past.

Casey sat on the bed's edge, fussing, tucking the covers around her sister, telling her it was going to be okay.

"I'll go downstairs," Marcus said, needing to distance himself from the closeness the two women shared. It was something he'd had once, lost, then forgotten, and would rather not remember. "I'll make sure the house is secure for the night." He checked the lock on the window, took a look at the ground below. "For what it's worth, I don't think he'll try again tonight. Finding me here was a big surprise. He'll need to factor that into his plans now. He won't try again until he's had time to do that."

Blinking slowly, as if she were coming out of a slumber, Laura stared at him. Gradually a frown appeared between her brows. "You're not just my sister's new boyfriend, are you, Marcus?"

When Marcus didn't answer, Laura looked at her sister instead. "Casey?"

Casey sighed. "No. He's not. He's here to protect you, Laura, until I can fix this thing. Whatever it is."

"No! Casey, I asked you to stay out of this. God, I couldn't bear it if you got hurt or—or worse, because of me! I don't want you involved. Or you, either, Marcus. Please, just—"

"I'm already involved, sis, so you're too late. I'm going to get you through this, and there's nothing more to say about it. As for Marcus, well, this sort of thing is…is…"

"It's what I do," Marcus supplied. He moved back to the bedside and met Laura's eyes. "And I'm very good at it, Laura. You're going to be okay, and so is your sister—providing she learns to do what she's told."

He searched Casey's eyes from the opposite side of the bed but could see no emotion in them aside from concern for her sister.

Laura sighed. "I should just leave. It would be better for everyone if I—"

"No, Laura," Casey said. "What would be better for everyone would be if you'd just tell us what's going on. Honey, for God's sake, you've been keeping your secrets for far too long. They're dangerous. You know that."

"They're not dangerous to you unless you know

them, Casey.'' Laura clamped her jaw tight and closed her eyes. "I'll sleep better knowing you're here, though, Marcus. Thank you for that."

"You're welcome," he told her. Then he looked at Casey.

"I'll stay with her until she falls asleep," she said.

He nodded. "I'll be downstairs." He backed out of the room, but when he got into the hallway, he leaned against the wall and closed his eyes. Dammit, what was happening to him? He'd made up his mind to get away from Casey and her sister as fast as he could, and now he was neck-deep in whatever trouble they were facing. Worse than that, he cared about them.

Both of them.

Nine

"Here," Casey said as she handed Laura a mild sleeping pill and a glass of water. "You'll never get any rest otherwise."

"I'm almost afraid to go to sleep."

"You don't have to be. Not with Marcus here."

Laura nodded, popped the pill into her mouth and took a sip of water to wash it down. Then she lay back on the pillows. "He's something, isn't he? That guy had to be twice his size, but he tossed him around like nothing."

"It was pretty impressive."

"It was amazing," Laura said. She sighed, searched her sister's face. "So, what about you two?"

"What *about* us?"

Laura managed to smile despite the fear she must still be feeling. "You know what I mean. Was it all for my benefit, or is there really something going on between you?"

Casey sighed, lowering her head. "He just found out I was a reporter today," she said.

Frowning, Laura whispered, "So?"

"So, I deliberately kept that from him. He hates reporters, and I knew he'd never agree to help us if I told him the truth." She shook her head slowly.

"Now he thinks I set this whole thing up just so I could do a story on him."

"But why would he think...oh my God. Casey! He's the Guardian, isn't he!"

Casey closed her eyes, bit her lip. Dammit, she'd done it again. She'd promised Marcus she wouldn't tell Laura, and now Laura knew and he'd be furious all over again.

"I wasn't supposed to know, was I."

Casey shook her head.

"It's okay, sis. I'll pretend I'm clueless. Oh Lord, you didn't even know what he looked like until I snapped the light on the other night! Did you? It all makes sense now. The way he reacted, looking so shocked and everything. And—and then he kissed the daylights out of you—or maybe it was you kissing the daylights out of him."

Casey nodded. "I—I don't know what came over me."

"I do. You like this guy, Casey. Admit it."

Closing her eyes slowly, she lowered her head. "I do. I don't know what it is about him, but it was happening even before I'd seen him in the light. I just...I don't know."

"You've got it bad for him, Casey."

Casey shook her head in denial, but in her heart she knew it was a lie. She wanted Marcus, but it was more than that.

It scared her.

"It's not like that," she said.

"Then what is it like?"

Shrugging, Casey tried to put her thoughts into

words. "He's keeping all kinds of secrets. He's like a mystery waiting to be solved, you know? I just…I'm just curious. That's all."

"You never could resist a mystery." Laura's eyes fell closed, then slowly opened again. "But there's more. Isn't there, Casey?"

Casey nodded. "There's more. He's hurting, too. It's all wrapped up in the secrets he's keeping. But it's a deep pain, and it's eating him up inside."

"You always want to make things better. Fix everything. Even this mess I'm in. So you think you can take care of his hurt?"

"I know I can."

"But does he?"

Casey shook her head. "He's got himself all locked up in a cage. Lives in self-imposed solitude. Doesn't want or need anyone's help. So I guess that's that."

"Yeah, right. And you're a pacifist." Her eyes fell closed again. "The guy doesn't stand a chance, sis. And if you ask me, he doesn't know how lucky he is."

Casey shook her head even as her sister drifted off to sleep. "No, I can't be thinking that way. I have to pull back. Take care of myself, you know?" Laura didn't answer, but it didn't matter. She was speaking more to herself now than to Laura, anyway. "I can't let this thing go any further. I mean, it would be just like me to go and do something stupid—like fall in love with him." Closing her eyes, she sighed deeply. "God, I could fall in love with him so easily. But I can't let that happen. I can't, because he's made it pretty clear how he feels. He likes his life the way it is. He doesn't want a relationship, doesn't even believe in love. I'd be stupid to set myself up for a heartbreak like that.''

She got to her feet slowly and paced toward the doorway. ''But I still think I can help him. And I should. I mean, he wouldn't take a dime for what he's doing for us—risking his life just to help us out. I owe him for that.''

Marcus was walking to the bedroom when he heard words that made him go utterly still. ''God, I could fall in love with him so easily,'' Casey said. ''But I can't let that happen.''

He blinked in shock and turned around, reversed his steps, wound up back in the living room pacing like a caged lion. He should run. Every cell in him was screaming at him to run.

But he thought about Laura's big ebony eyes and pale, frightened countenance. And then he thought about Casey's kiss. And he knew he couldn't. He was trapped right here until this thing ended.

One way...or another.

He was still pacing when Casey came back downstairs. His skin felt damp and prickly. It seemed too cold in here, and a dull throb worked its way up the back of his neck into the base of his skull. He couldn't remember feeling the physical symptoms of nervousness or panic ever before. But he felt them now. It was almost funny. He'd taken on armed assailants one by one or six at a time. But he was afraid to face down one small woman. Yeah. Funny. But he wasn't laughing.

"Thank you."

It was all she said. She stood at the bottom of the stairs, meeting his gaze from across the room. Her doe brown hair was tousled, and her eyes showed signs of the strain she'd been under. She looked tired, looked like she'd been tired and worried for quite some time, and he wondered how he'd missed it before.

"Don't thank me. He got away. I'm still kicking myself for that."

Pursing her lips, she came closer. He stood where he was, wary, wondering if she'd touch him and what he would do if she did. She didn't, as it turned out. She stopped halfway, stood awkwardly for a moment. "He got away," she said. "But not with my sister. If I'd been here alone, I don't think I could have stopped him."

"No, but you'd have tried, wouldn't you?"

Her brows lifted. "I'd have been on him like a rash. He'd have had to take the both of us."

"He'd have killed you."

She blinked but said nothing.

"He had a gun, you know."

"No. I didn't see one so I assumed—"

"Assuming is always a mistake. Usually a deadly one. He had a gun, just never got the chance to pull it."

"So you saved my life as well as Laura's." She lowered her head. "Words seem pretty shallow, Marcus. Thanking you...it doesn't even come close."

"Not necessary. It's what I do."

"I know, but—"

"Let me keep doing it."

She frowned at him. "What?"

"If you want to thank me, do it by keeping my secrets, Casey. Don't write the article. Let me keep doing what I do."

Slowly she released all her breath as her head tipped back and her eyes fell closed. "I never intended to write any article about you," she told him. "Never. I wish you could believe me."

"So do I."

Her head came down fast, and she met his eyes. "You can, Marcus. Look, take a look at my columns. For two years I've been exposing people's secrets, but only when those secrets caused harm. Politicians on the take or on drugs, or using public money to fund their mistresses and vacations. Dishonest judges, corrupt cops, scam artists. Don't think for a minute, though, that those are the only secrets I've been privy to. People tell me things, Marcus. Sometimes they tell me just to hear themselves talk, and sometimes they think they can use me for revenge. I've known about scandals that would turn your raven hair white, things that would have sold papers, things involving local celebrities. But I never printed them, because those secrets were hurting no one. No one but the people keeping them, that is."

He watched her as she delivered her little speech. And oddly enough, he found himself wanting to believe her. "That's a lot to swallow, coming from a journalist."

She nodded. "I know it is. But your secret is safe

with me, Marcus. Because it isn't a secret that's causing harm. Except to you.''

"To me?"

She nodded, started closer, then seemed to think better of it. Biting her lip, she walked to the sofa and sat down instead. It made him wonder what she'd intended when she'd taken that impulsive step toward him.

"It's no good, this life of secrets you're living. You've isolated yourself from the rest of the world. Don't you get lonely?"

Those eyes of hers, brown as velvet, seemed to draw emotions out of some hidden cauldron inside him. Feelings he hadn't even been aware of until she'd coaxed them to the surface.

"Lonely," he heard himself whisper, "is easier." And somehow, he forgot to keep his distance. Before he could think better of it, he'd joined her on the sofa.

"Easier than what?"

He blinked, thought about what he'd said and gave his head a shake. "Nothing. I'm tired...not thinking about what I'm saying."

"With people like you, Marcus, that's the best time to talk. It's the only time every word isn't carefully selected to conceal the truth. Those things that slip out...they're the most honest words you say."

"Are you a journalist or a shrink?"

She shrugged. "I don't usually get so philosophical. Only with you."

"Why do you suppose that is?"

She smiled at him, and his heart skipped a beat. Her face lit up a little. "That was really clever, turning the conversation around like that. You're good at it."

"You think so?"

"Mmm-hmm. But I'm better. And I think that when you said being lonely was easier, you meant it was easier than heartbreak and devastation. The things you felt when you lost your little sister, your family."

He shrugged and looked away. "If that is what I meant—and I'm not saying it is—then you have to admit it's accurate."

She turned slightly sideways on the sofa, so she faced him, and again her eyes dug into his soul. "Loneliness might be preferable to heartbreak, Marcus, but those aren't the only two options."

"Aren't they?"

Smiling very gently, she shook her head. "You know they aren't."

"For me they are. Caring…getting involved…is always a risk. No matter how careful you are, how cautiously you go into it, there's still a chance it will fall apart in the end."

"And there's an equal chance it could turn out to be wonderful."

"Not worth the risk."

"And growing old alone is a better option?"

He lowered his head. They were dancing all around it, but he knew what she was talking about. Not just any relationship, but one with her. He'd heard what she'd said upstairs. He knew. "If you'd ever had your soul ripped right out of your body, Casey, you wouldn't have to ask. Anything—*anything*—is preferable to that."

Her hand, trembling slightly, touched his face. A touch as light as an angel's sigh. "I don't think I've ever known anyone to hurt as much as you do."

He tried not to take so much comfort in the feel of her fingers, inching into his hair, moving in small circles on his scalp. Almost as if she were unconsciously trying to rub his pain away.

"My hurt is in the past," he told her. "All I want is to keep it there."

"If you only knew how wrong that is."

He brought his head up, and as he did, her gentle touch fell away. "Wrong? About wanting to keep the worst pain of my life in the past?"

"It isn't in the past. It's with you every day of your life. For God's sake, Marcus, it's in everything you do. That dark coat—that secret identity you cling to—it isn't a disguise, it's a shield."

He shook his head. "No. One thing has nothing to do with the other."

She met his eyes and without a word told him she thought he was wrong about that. The problem was, she was right. He knew it. He'd always known it. The other problem was, he couldn't look away from her, and she must see the truth as clearly in his eyes as he could see the knowledge in hers.

He didn't like her knowing so much…about him, about his secrets. His innermost feelings. His demons.

"You know," she said, "if you talked about what happened, it might help."

Still her eyes plumbed his. Explored the deepest

parts of his soul, places even he no longer visited. "No." A single word, but his tone said more. It said, "No trespassing. Sacred ground. Absolutely no admittance."

And she heard it. She lowered her eyes, stopped her foray into his forest of illusion.

"I'm not going to push."

"I wasn't going to let you."

Her smile was slight, unplanned, and it didn't quite reach her eyes. "I'm pretty good at pushing. I doubt you could stop me."

"Don't kid yourself, Casey. If I could handle that bald-headed lug who tried to run off with your sister, I think I can handle you."

Her head came up slowly, eyes locking on his. But they were dark now. Smoky. "You think so?" she whispered.

Oh, hell. He swallowed hard, reminded himself that he wasn't going to let this happen. He'd decided it was a bad idea. That a one-night stand with her was far too dangerous to risk. That...

Her eyes held his, drew him closer. He had no choice. It wasn't a mental thing, it was purely physical, and as impossible to resist as gravity. And so he went, closer, and pressed his mouth to hers. And his thought processes ended the second he felt that soft yielding of her lips. Their gentle parting. Their moistness. The voice of reason, of logic vanished. Alarm bells faded. Desire took over.

He wrapped his arms around her, because she just wasn't close enough to him. One arm extended the length of her back, and his palm cupped her head.

Better. He could kiss her more thoroughly this way. And he did. He held her face to his and invaded her mouth with his tongue. A soft sound of yearning escaped from her mouth into his and made his pulse skyrocket. The warm, tight skin of her waist heated his other palm, where he'd slipped it beneath her blouse. He tightened his hold, tilted his head and kept plumbing the moist recesses of her mouth. His head cycloned, and the touch of her fingers burying themselves in his hair only heightened the effect.

He eased her backward, moving with her. Her breasts were pressed to his chest, her back sinking into the cushions. Hands caressing him, his shoulders, his back, his buttocks, sent him into some other realm. One where nothing existed beyond her mouth, her hands, her body stretched beneath his. He nudged her thighs apart and nestled his hips tight against her, and she clenched her fingers to pull him closer. The thunder of her heart hypnotized him, drew him into her rhythm. His lips trailed from her mouth to her jaw and lower. The pulse in her throat fluttering against his mouth sent him up in flames. He heard a deep moan and realized the sound came from his own lips.

And then her hands were on his shoulders. Her voice, as breathless and hoarse as if she'd just run a marathon, filled his ears. "Marcus, I told myself I wouldn't let this happen...."

"So did I."

He worked his way to her mouth again, kissed her until she managed to turn her head. "I...we should...stop."

"I don't want to stop."

"I don't, either, but, Marcus…"

He heard the plea in her voice, forced himself to slow down, take a full breath, look into her eyes. He didn't find them wide or frightened. Only hooded and glazed with passion. But even so, she whispered, "I want you more than I want to draw another breath, Marcus. But I—"

Closing his eyes, he finished for her. "You don't do one-night stands."

"It goes way beyond that, and I think you know it."

He did. He gently eased his weight from her, then closed his hands on her shoulders and drew her upright again. Heart still pounding, he smoothed her tousled hair with his palms and wondered how she managed to make it feel like silk and smell like wild strawberries.

"It would mean too much, Marcus. You say you're incapable of feeling anything for me. But I'm not incapable. I *can* feel. And if we…if we do this…I will."

He let his eyes roam her face. Traced the line of her jaw and the fullness of her lips. Delved into those incredibly huge brown eyes. He wanted her. And it was more than physical. "You're a smart lady."

"Too smart to let you break my heart."

He forced himself to take his hands away, to stop stroking her hair. "Go on up to bed, Casey. I'll, uh, I'll be down here if you need me."

"If I change my mind," she corrected him.

"Yeah. And, uh, if you don't…maybe you'd best lock your door."

She smiled. Nervous, trembling, still aroused. "I trust you, Marcus."

"I'm not sure I trust myself." He tried to smile, but it felt false, tight. "Besides, I might sleepwalk."

She got to her feet, stumbled. Marcus reacted fast, springing up himself to steady her. Then he wished he hadn't, because she lowered her head to his chest and emitted a shuddery sigh. Gripping her shoulders, he set her gently away from him. "Good night, Casey." She blinked at him, looking hurt, so he added, "I'm only human."

Understanding dawned. She nodded, turned away. "Good night, Marcus," she whispered. And she crossed the room, went up the stairs, never looked back.

Marcus watched her all the way to the top, then he lowered his head, closed his eyes and swore until he ran out of breath.

Ten

Marcus thought dying couldn't feel much worse than watching Casey go up those stairs. He had to do something, take some action, both to protect Casey and Laura and to distance himself from them.

It was Saturday tomorrow, and they wouldn't be going to work. He'd have to stick close…they were entirely too vulnerable in the house by themselves. He didn't like it, any of it. The risk to Laura and to Casey. Being put in the position of having to stay so close. Unable to run the way his instincts were insisting he do.

He sat on the edge of the sofa, head in his hands. Sweating. Shaking. How could one woman reduce him to this? How could he want her so much?

Maybe it was as simple as knowing he couldn't have her. Maybe that was what was making him so crazy. He couldn't have her. She'd told him straight-out that she didn't do one-night stands. She wanted a relationship. Some kind of sign on his part that a commitment wasn't out of the question. She wanted caring, trust, a sort of closeness he hadn't shared with anyone since…

Since that day. He squeezed his eyes tighter. He wasn't going to think about that. Relive it. Not again.

His eyes burned, and he got up to pace, just to keep himself from falling asleep. Last night he'd been on duty, guarding the two women. Today, Graham's news had kept him restless, and he'd never once closed his eyes. Tonight wouldn't be any better. His head ached from sleep deprivation and his eyes blurred. He paced back to the sofa and sat down. Let his head fall back against the cushions.

The memories closed in, his deepest terror coming to life again. He fought it. God, if this wasn't hell, he didn't know what was. To be robbed of nearly every memory of his childhood—except for a few snatches that appeared all too briefly, fleeting glimpses of the love he must have known once. And one nightmare. In all its gory detail.

He knew something was wrong the second his father came through the door. His normally ruddy face was white, his eyes—they just looked so frightened.

"Dad?"

He'd pushed past Marcus, shouting for the others. And Marcus's mother rushed in from the kitchen, where she'd been looking for Sara. Sara...playing that stupid hide-and-seek game of hers and making his mom nuts because she couldn't find her.

"Get some things together," his father said. Even his voice sounded funny. Marcus got a tight feeling in his chest. "We have to leave, right now. Where's Sara?"

"I'll get her."

Marcus frowned as his mom hurried off, calling Sara's name. She hadn't even asked what was wrong.

Why his dad was so upset. It was as if she already knew. As if she'd been expecting this.

And maybe she had. Even Marcus knew his dad's "business" wasn't an honest one. He'd heard his mother condemn it often enough, plead with him to get out. Even their cousins in Texas disapproved, though they tried not to let it show. Marcus wished he'd tried to find out more...he only knew it involved money. Suitcases full of it sometimes. He'd thought he didn't want to know more, but now he knew he had to.

"Dad, what's going on?"

"Not now, Marcus."

"Yes. Now. Tell me, why do you look so scared? What's happening?"

His father looked at him for the first time, and Marcus saw the fear more than ever. "It's gonna be okay. Your old man screwed up, Marc, but it's not going to happen again. Not ever again, I promise."

"But—"

Reaching down, his father rumpled Marcus's hair. "I need you to help, Marcus. Go down to the cellar and bring up those old suitcases your mom keeps there, okay?"

"Down to the cellar?" Marcus glanced toward the doorway. It was dark in the cellar. He'd always hated the dark. But then he looked up at his dad again and saw that his father was a lot more afraid of whatever was happening than Marcus was of the dark, damp cellar. So he lifted his chin and nodded hard, and then he turned and went down those rickety stairs.

He'd barely got down them when he heard the

crash—like someone smashing through the front door. Whirling to run back upstairs, he glimpsed his father's large hand shoving the cellar door closed. And then he heard that horrible sound—the rapid, staccato explosions of gunfire. Like in some kind of gangster movie.

He froze on the stairs. Just froze there. And the sounds went on, and he told himself to run up there, to do something, to help his family. But his feet refused to move. His entire body was utterly paralyzed. He didn't even think he was breathing while those machine guns went on and on.

And then he heard his mother's scream...a name...

What was the name, what was the name?

His hands pressed to his ears, and it was a long time before he took them away again to realize the gunfire had stopped. There was nothing but silence upstairs now. Was he still there—the man with the deadly gun? Had he left? Or was he waiting? What about Mom? Dad?

Sara!

Oh God, little Sara!

Finally the feeling came back into his limbs, and Marcus got his body to move. He crept up the stairs, silently, pushed on the door. Very slowly, it opened...revealing a nightmare.

The smells hit him first. The sulfury scent the gun had left behind. And something else. Something...something bad.

Then he blinked and stepped into the living room, turning his head slowly. Seeing the blood. Spatters of it on every wall. Even some on the ceiling. The light fixture. And there was more than blood. There were...things...

He quickly lowered his head, only to see a pool of blood on the floor underneath his feet. And when he looked away from that, he saw another pool, near the kitchen, and long, streaked trails leading from each stain to the still-open front door.

He swallowed hard and tried to call his mom, his dad. But when he moved his mouth, only a dry gust of wind came out. He couldn't make a sound. The walls were riddled with holes. The mirror was in glittering silver fragments on the floor. Stuffing bled through the holes in the sofa.

He walked slowly through his house, his home, and he searched for his family. But he already knew he wouldn't find them.

He'd been afraid of the cellar...afraid of the dark. Now he realized it had been the only safe place in the entire house. Maybe...maybe it was the only safe place in the world. Right now he wanted to go back into the darkness and never, ever come out into the light again.

He stepped out of the house into the street, and he heard sirens. But he didn't care about them. He needed to get away from the house and the sounds ringing in his ears. Gunfire, his mother's scream. Away, away, away...into the dark.

"No. No, dammit, no."

"Marcus..."

He opened his eyes. Sunlight streamed through the windows and shone in his eyes. Leaning over him, an angel. Fawn hair surrounded by a nimbus of sunlight behind her. Eyes as deep as heaven. Petal-soft hand, stroking his face.

"Are you all right?" she whispered.

He blinked, looked around him. No bullet holes. No blood. He was an adult, not a helpless, terrified ten-year-old. He was in Casey's house, not his childhood home. He was doing a job. He'd only been dreaming.

Dreaming... Sleeping!

His eyes widened. "I fell asleep! Laura—"

"She's fine. It's you I'm worried about."

Marcus sat up, tried to clear his head. It ached, and he closed his eyes slowly. "You have any coffee?"

"Marcus, you're changing the subject." Those probing eyes were deadly, and they saw way too much as they searched his face. "You were having a nightmare."

"Nightmare, memory. Call it what you will." He ran a hand over his face, and it met stubble. He must look like a bum by now. He needed to shave. "It's nothing that hasn't happened before, Casey. Not a big deal, okay?"

She frowned. "You have this dream often?"

He nodded, then stopped himself. "Only since my tenth Christmas." He bit his lip, gave his head a shake. "It doesn't matter."

"It does to me."

He finally met her steady gaze and knew she meant what she said. "It shouldn't, Casey."

She looked away, hurt maybe, but then he'd meant her to be. At least the message was received. A not-so-gentle reminder that it would do her no good to let herself care about him, because he could never return the feelings. He intended to see to it she didn't forget.

"How about that coffee?"

"Somebody say coffee?" Laura appeared in the doorway from the kitchen with a tray balanced in her hands. Smiling, she carried it in and set it on the coffee table. Three steaming mugs, cream, sugar, spoons and a plate of pastries that smelled so good Marcus almost forgot about the bad dreams.

"You're a mind reader," he said.

"Nope. I just like to eat." She smiled at him.

Marcus found himself admiring her spunk. To wake up this bright-eyed after the night she'd had. "You look rested."

"Casey slipped me a Mickey last night. I figured she had plans she'd rather I slept through." Laura winked at her sister.

"I gave her a sleeping pill, and she needed it."

"I agree with you there," Marcus said, and he reached for a cup of coffee while eyeing the pastries. "I hardly deserve this after falling asleep on the job."

"Fine," Laura said. "I'll just eat them myself."

"No you won't." Marcus grabbed a Danish, while Casey quickly snatched a muffin.

"You needed the rest, too," Laura said, taking a doughnut and a blueberry muffin both in one hand, her coffee in the other, and settling down in a chair. "You don't seem like the type who'd doze unintentionally otherwise."

"Needed or not, I should have been awake."

"Yeah," Casey said. "And the sleep didn't get you much rest anyway, did it?"

Laura frowned at him. "What? Why not?"

He shook his head. "Nothing. Forget it."

But now it was Laura's ebony gaze searching his face instead of Casey's brown one. She frowned hard. "Gee, you don't look so good this morning. You sure that big lug didn't get a piece of you last night?"

"Not on his best day."

For some reason that comment made both women smile. He chose to ignore their apparent amusement, and he munched on his Danish for a while. Then he went on. "I've been thinking, and I've decided it's no longer feasible for you two to stay here."

The light in Laura's eyes faded a little. Casey just stared at him. "Marcus, that's why you're here. To keep Laura safe."

"That's not going to work anymore. This guy, whoever he is, knows I'm here now. He'll just watch, wait until I'm not around and make his move. It isn't worth the risk to either of you."

Casey sighed but nodded. "I guess you do have a point. And you can't guard us twenty-four-seven, after all."

"No, I can't."

"So where do we go?" Laura asked.

"I'm working on that."

"I might have a few ideas," Casey said. "Let me work on it today. But, Marcus, I have to tell you, I really don't think this is a good idea."

"I didn't think you would. And I suppose you have a dozen reasons why not."

She tilted her head. "Only one, really. If we go into hiding, the problem isn't solved. It's only postponed. We have to come home sooner or later, and when we do, the jerk will be here waiting." She lowered her head and sighed deeply. When she raised it again, she faced her sister. "Laura, if you'd just tell us—"

"No, I can't." Laura set her cup down carefully. "Casey, you're already in danger because of me. You could get hurt anytime, caught in the crossfire. But if you know any more than you already do, you might become a target, too, and I'm not willing to see that happen." She closed her eyes slowly. "I should just leave…"

"I'd rather let them shoot me than lose you, Laura."

When Laura's eyes opened again they were wet. Marcus felt his own grow hot and damp. He'd die to save little Sara if he had it to do over. He knew exactly what Casey meant.

"When I catch him, Laura," he said gently, "and I *will* catch him, we're going to find out the truth anyway."

"When you catch him, it won't matter. He'll be in prison where he can't hurt either of you."

She made sense. He hated to admit it, but she did. "Okay, so you're not talking. I can respect that…for now."

"At least you didn't say, 'Vee have vays of making you talk,'" she said, a false lightness to her voice. She glanced around the room a bit nervously, brushing the crumbs from her fingers. "So when can we get out of here?"

"Right now, if you want," Marcus told her. It was obvious she was still afraid. "I'll take you both to the hotel where I'm staying. Introduce you to Graham."

Laura's head came up. "Graham? Is he your sidekick?"

Marcus only frowned.

"Well, every superhero has one, right?"

He shot Casey a look, saw her grimace. Then he glanced at Laura again. "I'm no superhero, Laura. What gave you that idea?"

She shrugged, not quite meeting his gaze. "You saved my life last night," she told him. "That makes you a hero in my book."

His face heated, and he had to lower his head.

"Okay, then," Casey said, getting quickly to her feet and gathering up the mugs and tray. "You go on to meet the mysterious sidekick at the hotel with Marcus. I'll meet you there later."

Marcus felt alarms going off. "You're not coming with us?"

She didn't look him in the eye. "I have a couple of things to do first. At the office, work stuff. You know."

He wondered if that "work stuff" involved him. He still wasn't certain he could trust her. She could ruin him with one article.

She looked him in the eye then. Briefly. But he saw her promise there as clearly as if she'd spoken it aloud. And he found himself believing her. Dangerous thing to do, a little voice whispered.

"Okay," he said, despite the nagging doubts. "Do what you have to, Casey."

"I'll meet you in time for lunch. Promise."

"If you're late, I'll assume you're in trouble and come looking."

She smiled then. Blinked fast, and averted her face. He wondered why. "I won't be late," she whispered.

What had he said? Why did she look like that?

She carried the tray to the kitchen, and he heard water running. As soon as she was out of sight, Laura leaned close. "That was pretty romantic, what you just said."

Frowning, Marcus shook his head. "What did I say?"

Laura rolled her eyes. "You mean it wasn't intentional?"

"How could it have been when I don't even know what you're talking about?"

"So you aren't deliberately trying to sweep my big sister off her feet?"

He stared at her in astonishment.

Laura shrugged. "For a clueless male, you're doing a pretty good job of it." She got to her feet. "I'm going to throw some things in a bag for Casey and me. Five minutes, okay?"

"Sure." He watched her go and sat there wondering what the hell had just happened. It most certainly was *not* his intention to sweep Casey off her feet, as her sister so eloquently put it. Hell, he was trying to keep her from caring about him. What had he done wrong?

Minutes later, Casey was back, wiping her hands

on a dishtowel. Laura trotted down the stairs with a bulging satchel. Marcus got up to take the bag and walked both women outside.

She knew the year now. The year of Marcus's nightmare. He'd talked a little too much when he woke up. She'd like to think that was because he was beginning to trust her, just a little. She didn't imagine he trusted too many people.

But the nightmare of his youth had happened when he was ten years old. Around Christmas. And he'd told her he was thirty-two now, so that made it 1976. She wasn't certain of the locale but guessed it was in or near Silver City, since he seemed to have been there ever since. So she returned to the newspaper and logged into the annals of the *Silver City Times,* and she pored over every one of the fifty-two weekly issues from that year.

Finally she found it.

December 23, 1976.

A family of four was apparently murdered in a gangland-style shooting early this afternoon. Silver City police, responding to a neighbor's report of gunshots, arrived at the home of John Brand to find evidence of a struggle inside. Though he refused to give us the nature of the evidence, Sergeant William Hammersmith of SCPD says it's obvious there were multiple gunshot victims and that their bodies had been removed from the premises, probably by the unknown assailant. Missing and presumed dead are John Brand, his wife, Sally Brand, and their two children, Marcus, ten, and Sara, four. A massive search for the bodies of the victims is already under way, Hammersmith said.

John Brand worked as an accountant and, according to D.A. Richard Kendall, was suspected to have connections with organized crime figures in the area. Sergeant Hammersmith confirms that the shootings at 24 Ivy Lane have all the markings of a professional hit.

Casey read and then reread the article. No photos. But there was no doubt this must be Marcus's family. Only the story was flawed. Marcus hadn't been killed. He'd survived somehow. God, how? Where had he gone? How had he managed all alone in the world at such a tender age?

"No wonder he's so isolated. So determined to be a loner."

As she printed a copy of the article, she thought what an odd coincidence it was that his last name was Brand. There were Brands right here in Texas, in nearby Quinn. They'd been friends of her parents' for as long as she could remember. She still exchanged Christmas cards with them, and they usually dropped a note a couple of times a year, asking about her and Laura. How they were doing and so on.

Strange. She paused, staring at the printout, her mind whirling. Hadn't Marcus said something about having been in Texas before? What if these Brands were some relation of his? God, did they even know he was alive?

She quickly skimmed through the newspapers that came after the December 23 one, perusing every page of print in search of a follow-up story. Surely the killer had been caught....

No. No, by the looks of things, he had never been found. There was only one further mention of the murders, when the bodies of Sally and John Brand had been discovered in a nearby river. But the children's bodies had not been found. Police surmised that as a final act of cruelty, the killer had dumped the bodies in separate areas, and suggested the bodies of the children might never be recovered.

"Of course they won't," Casey muttered. "Not Marcus's, at least. Because he wasn't killed. He lived. Somehow he lived...*with the nightmares.*"

Casey printed that article up, as well, and added both to her growing file on the man Silver City called the Guardian. A man living a lie, all to protect his shattered heart from being broken again.

She blinked tears from her eyes and glanced at her watch. She'd better run or she'd be late for lunch.

And he'd come looking.

The thought brought a tight pain to her heart and a bittersweet smile to her lips.

Eleven

Marcus paced, his shoes making odd tracks on the wet floor near the pool. A four-star restaurant available, and Laura had insisted on lunch beside the hotel's indoor pool. Sunlight shone through the glass walls surrounding them, and there were even umbrella-shaded tables and a couple of potted palms to complete the tropical illusion.

"Not exactly in keeping with the holiday spirit, Miss Jones," Graham chuckled. Laura was climbing out of the pool, dripping wet, and Graham met her halfway with a towel. If he'd been forty years younger, Marcus thought his old friend would be falling in love. Maybe he was, anyway. He certainly seemed smitten.

"Don't tell me you'd rather eat lunch in that stuffy room?"

"Suite, dear. It's a suite."

"Yeah, penthouse suite, too." She waved one hand as if cooling her face. "Business must be good, huh? But even you rich guys have to get out once in a while."

"Indeed."

Marcus watched Laura as she made her way to the table while vigorously toweling dry. Then he resumed pacing. Casey wasn't back yet. She should be. And he shouldn't be this worried. Yes, if it was anyone else, he'd be getting a bit concerned at this point. But he wouldn't feel this same sick ball of dread in his stomach. Or this jerky convulsion of his heart every time he heard footsteps in the foyer.

"I would have thought," Graham said, "you might have preferred the hotel restaurant. It's quite nice, you know."

"Yeah, if you like tinsel and pinecones hanging from every corner, not to mention the stupid red hats the waitresses are all wearing."

Marcus glanced her way, the topic catching his attention. "Don't forget the piped-in carols."

Laura rolled her eyes at him. "Don't remind me."

Graham stared from one of them to the other. Then did so again. "I, er, take it you don't particularly enjoy the holiday season, Miss Jones?"

"Call me Laura, okay?"

Graham smiled, clearly besotted. "Of course."

"It's just not my favorite time of year."

"It isn't mine, either," Marcus said. "And frankly, I'm sick of people thinking that's strange."

"Me, too. But right now I'd wrestle Rudolph for a cheeseburger. Where *is* that waiter?"

"Maybe he vanished with your sister. She seems to be running a little late herself."

Laura gripped Graham's arm and twisted it around so she could see his watch. "Five after twelve. Uh-oh—"

"Five after? I have noon on the nose." Marcus

tapped his watch, shook his head. "That's it, I'm going over there."

"Me, too."

"Stay here, Laura. It could be dangerous. Graham will watch you, and if anything's happened to Casey, I'll—"

"You'll what?"

Marcus spun to see Casey standing in the entryway, arms crossed over her chest. The air rushed out of him, along with the tension that had been building steadily ever since she'd left his sight this morning. "You're late."

"By mere seconds," she said.

"I was on my way to track you down."

"So I gathered." She smiled, lowered her head. "Thanks for that."

Frowning, Marcus got the feeling the conversation was sailing way over his head...again. "There's no need to thank me. I said I would. I was getting worried."

Smiling even more, she said, "I know. Thanks for that, too."

He shook his head, half-convinced they were speaking two different languages. He searched his brain for a reply but couldn't think of a thing to say.

She came the rest of the way in, and when she passed him, she passed close. Almost close enough to brush against him, but not quite. The space of a breath remained between them. Just enough to make him wish it didn't. And maybe that was deliberate.

"You must be Graham," she said, smiling and extending a hand.

He rose, took her hand, nodded deeply. "Ms. Jones."

"Call her Casey," Laura instructed. "Where is that waiter? I'm starving."

"You're always starving," Casey told her. She nodded at her sister's dripping hair. "What's this, a Christmas swim?"

"Bah!"

"Humbug," Marcus said at the same moment.

Casey's frown puzzled him. He thought the simultaneous grinching was rather funny himself. She looked...odd. Deep in thought. But in a second she gave her head a shake and snapped herself out of whatever had come over her.

Then the waiter finally arrived. Laura had preordered for everyone, protesting only mildly when Marcus told her to get whatever she wanted on him. He suspected she'd secretly relished the opportunity.

The choices told him he'd suspected right. Stuffed crab, glazed asparagus, Cornish game hens and assorted vegetables, accompanied by a bottle of imported wine and an entire cheesecake.

"My God, who ordered this mess? It's only lunch!" Casey said, wide-eyed.

Everyone looked at Laura. She only shrugged and dug in.

Casey shook her head. "It isn't fair. If I ate like that, I'd weigh a ton."

"Oh yeah, try to sound jealous, sis. When you're the one dating the super—" She stopped herself, bit her lip. "Supernice guy," she finished, but it was a lame attempt.

Marcus leaned back in the chair, having lost his appetite. "So you know."

Laura tried to look innocent with those huge black eyes, but it didn't fool him.

"Admit it, Laura. That's the second time you've referred to me as some kind of superhero, and while it's far from accurate, I can only imagine one way you might have got that idea into your head."

"The way you flipped that Neanderthal last night?" she asked, blinking like a doe in headlights.

He shook his head.

"I told her," Casey said.

"She did not! I guessed. She let something slip about you not liking the press, Marcus, and I just figured it out all by myself."

"Did you, now?"

Laura nodded. Casey looked as if she were losing her appetite.

"That the way it happened, Casey?"

"If I tell you it was, are you going to believe me?"

He narrowed his eyes on her. What kind of game was this?

"Never mind. I guess I have my answer." She swallowed hard and shoved her plate away.

"I don't have mine," he said.

"You do so, Marcus," Laura said, raising her voice now. "Hey, I'm talking to you!" She poked him in the shoulder, but he kept his eyes focused on Casey.

Casey stared right back. "I'm not going to do this. You either trust me, or you don't. And it's pretty obvious, Marcus, that you don't."

He said nothing.

"You're blowing it, Marc," Laura said.

"Big-time," Graham added.

But Marcus's focus was broken so suddenly he nearly felt it snap, and he turned to Laura. "What did you call me?"

She frowned, seeming to recall her words. Then she closed her eyes. "Sorry. It slipped out. It's a habit I have, shortening names. Drives some people nuts."

Graham cleared his throat. "Perhaps we ought to be working on a safe haven for the ladies. I've checked with the hotel, but they're completely booked."

"I don't want them in town, at any rate, Graham. It wouldn't take much work for this fellow to track them down, particularly if he's a professional—and I believe he is. Besides which, if this is going to work, I'll need to be out at the house, waiting for him to return. I can't be here watching the women."

"I think I have that particular problem solved," Casey said.

Everyone looked up expectantly, including Laura, who was still chewing.

"We have some old family friends in a nearby town. Very rural," Casey said. "Very safe."

"How can you be sure?" Marcus asked her.

"Still don't trust me, do you? Even on this? You think I'd stash my sister somewhere that wasn't safe?"

He sighed, lowered his head.

"The head of the household is the town sheriff. That good enough for you?"

Licking his lips, he faced her once more. Gazes

clashed, jet and brown, across the table. "I never said I didn't trust you."

"You didn't have to." But her tone was softer, her eyes a bit less hostile. "But I...think I understand."

He didn't like that. Not a bit. "Don't try to analyze me, Casey."

"Scares you, does it?"

He heard Graham try to suppress a chuckle and fail.

"Where is this place?" he asked.

"I'll give you directions on the way," she told him. "You ready?"

"I doubt it."

"So do I."

Her eyes hid a thousand secrets, and every sentence she uttered could have as many meanings. She was maddening. "Your things are upstairs," he said finally.

"Gee, talk about tension!" Laura's sarcasm was evident.

"One could scarcely cut it with a chain saw," Graham commented.

"Well, I'll get our stuff," Laura said. "I need to change anyway."

"Not alone, you won't." Casey got up, and together the women left.

"Neither of them should probably go about unaccompanied, Marcus," Graham said.

Marcus sighed. "I know. I'm right behind them, but I needed a minute. I want you to search their house while I'm gone."

Graham's scowl was clearly disapproving. "But... but why—whatever for?"

"Because I'm half-convinced Casey is gathering information on me for a story. She could destroy everything I've worked for—everything Caine worked for, and the Guardian before him."

"I seriously doubt—"

"I doubt it, too. Because I want to doubt it. But I can't take the risk, Graham. So search the place. Don't take anything. Just tell me what you find. Okay?"

Graham tapped his folded napkin against the table's edge. "I find it very distasteful, sir, but yes. I'll do as you ask."

"So it's 'sir' now?"

"Will there be anything else?"

Graham had turned to ice. Marcus could feel the chill from here. "No, Graham. Nothing else. I shouldn't be more than a few hours."

"Very well, sir," Graham said. "Have a pleasant trip." Marcus turned to leave, but before he'd gone ten steps, he could have sworn his old companion muttered something else. One more word. It sounded a lot like "fool."

Casey sat in the front seat, when she could just as easily have climbed into the back with her sister. She knew it was because she wanted to be close to him. It irritated her that he didn't trust her, but she told herself it would be tough for a man who'd seen the things he'd seen to trust anyone.

Although she sensed that wasn't the problem. He seemed to trust Graham. He could trust her, too, if he wanted to. No, the major wall standing between him and her was that he *didn't* want to. He didn't want to get close, didn't want to feel a thing for her, refused to let himself. Because he was scared. Scared half out of his mind, and he probably didn't even realize it.

She was curious about his connection—or lack thereof—to the Brands of Texas. It seemed like an odd coincidence that they shared a name, and that he'd mentioned visiting Texas in his childhood. But it might not be. It might be more than that. She supposed it was a pretty underhanded trick she was pulling here, bringing him to the Texas Brand to see his reaction to the place. But it truly was the only safe place she could think of to leave Laura.

Still, she could have warned him. She'd deliberately not mentioned the name. She wanted to see for herself how he responded to the place, the family. It would give her another clue about him, his past, his life, who he was inside.

And those were things she was longing to know for reasons she didn't even understand. Her curiosity— hell, she was used to that. But this was different. Not at all the same, not even originating from the same place in her body. The snoop in her came from some spot in her brain. But this—this came from somewhere deeper. Her gut. Her soul.

Her heart?

She swallowed hard and admitted to herself that it was entirely possible.

''Anything wrong, Casey?''

With the two-hour drive barely half over, she'd been thinking too much. Silence filled the car like an electrical charge—one that might spark and set them all alight if anyone spoke. Her relief when Marcus finally broke it made her sigh out loud.

"I really didn't mean to tell Laura about you," she said, conceding that maybe he did need to hear it from her.

"I know that."

She swung her head around, facing him, feeling her heart give a little flutter at the way the sun streamed through the windshield and made his dark hair gleam. His eyes, hidden behind sunglasses, gave him a mysterious air. Another disguise. And maybe he felt freer when he was protected by one, be it his fedora and trench coat, his secret identity or his shades.

"I shouldn't have been so rough on you over it. Laura's...pretty perceptive."

"Why, thank you," came a voice from the back seat.

Casey shot her a look, and Laura pouted. "You want I should ride in the trunk so you two can be alone? Gosh, sis, the man is *driving.*"

Casey lowered her head in exasperation while Marcus tried not to chuckle, failed and wound up laughing out loud.

"About time somebody around here lightened up," Laura muttered. "So, where are we going?"

Casey stiffened. "I, uh, want to surprise you."

Shrugging, Laura sharpened her gaze and stared out the window just as they passed a sign that said Quinn, forty miles. She settled back into her seat with a contented sigh. "Not much of a surprise, sis. We're going to the Brand ranch, aren't we?"

Marcus spun around so fast his arms moved with his head and the car careened into the other lane. "What did you say?"

"Marcus! The car!" Casey jerked the wheel toward her, and Marcus faced front, steered onto the shoulder and braked to a dusty stop.

"Sheesh," Laura said as she straightened in her seat. "What *did* I say?"

"Marcus, what just happened here?"

He closed his eyes, and his hands, where he gripped the wheel, were white.

Laura reached up from the back seat to clasp his shoulder. "It's no big deal, Marcus. We're going out to a ranch called the Texas Brand, out near Quinn. The Brands are...well, they're old friends."

"How old?" Marcus asked, still gripping the wheel. He opened his eyes but didn't look at either of them. His gaze was fixed on some invisible point straight ahead.

"My parents were friends of the Brands ever since I can remember, Marcus. I trust them. And I know Laura will be safe there." Casey spoke very slowly. She wondered if his reaction was due to the Brands having the same last name as him, or if it was something more. She touched his hand on the wheel, tight, hard, even cool. "Marcus, what's wrong?"

He searched her face then, reaching deep, and she knew he was trying to figure out whether she knew his name was Brand. Whether she'd set him up somehow or whether this truly was all just a coincidence. She could feel him searching her, and not finding any answers, and growing frustrated. And she felt as guilty as a thief for putting him through this.

But what if they were family? What if they really were? Everyone needed family. Especially at this time of the year.

He stared at her a long time and finally shook his head in defeat and turned away. Pulling the car back onto the road, he headed toward the Texas Brand.

It was coincidence, Marcus told himself. His memory, still so hazy, nonetheless tried to surface every once in a while. He'd prefer it didn't. His name, his true name, was Marcus Brand, not Marcus Caine. And he knew he'd come to a ranch in Texas, usually at Christmastime, to visit a large family. Vague impressions, out of order and unclear. Sometimes a face. Sometimes a voice. Horses. He remembered horses. And a porch swing Sara would never get out of.

But this couldn't be the same place, and these Brands who were old friends of the Joneses couldn't possibly be the same people. Because if they were, it couldn't be coincidence—and yet Casey had no way of knowing.

They rode in silence, Casey finally showing her frustration with every look, every sigh. She gave up and turned on the radio, tuning in to a rock station— not an easy find in rural West Texas. But she found one, blasting a popular song.

The frustration left her face. Marcus saw it, because he couldn't keep from looking at her every few seconds, no matter how strongly he suspected her of treachery. She was beautiful. Soft.

So he saw her brows go up. Saw her glance over the seat at her sister and wiggle them. Followed her gaze back there to see her sister wink and nod.

A second later, Casey and Laura were singing along to the radio. Full volume. Laughing out loud when they got the words wrong. Making up ludicrous lyrics to take the place of the real ones on occasion.

He couldn't think about Casey's hidden agenda or ulterior motives. Couldn't tune the girls out. Couldn't keep from looking at them, and his lips twitched and tugged into a reluctant grin. "You're both nuts."

He switched the radio off.

Casey and Laura kept singing anyway, finishing the song in spite of his wet-blanket routine.

They both seemed more relaxed when the final note, slightly off-key, died away and they leaned back against their seats, smiling. "You have to admit, it makes the ride go faster," Laura said.

"I think I could argue that point."

"Well, it's no fun if you don't sing along, silly. We do it all the time, don't we, Case?"

"All the time."

"Even with the windows down?" Marcus asked.

"Even at red lights with the windows down," Laura told him. "Remember, Casey, when the cop in the next lane started singing along?"

"I remember. I thought he was going to ticket us for noise pollution, and all of a sudden, he bursts into song. And he was *bad*."

"Worse than us," Laura said, nodding.

"He must have been pretty bad," Marcus said. Casey punched his shoulder lightly.

"Keep it up and we'll make you join the Jones family singers."

"We're almost there," Laura said, pointing. "Turn off here, Marcus. Gosh, I can't wait to see them. It's been so long." She leaned forward, her chin over the back of the seat between Marcus and Casey. "Do they know we're coming?"

"I spoke with Garrett this morning. He said the whole family would be there to greet us."

"He wasn't lying. Look!"

Marcus glanced in the direction Laura pointed. Beyond the towering wooden arch with Texas Brand carved into it, the driveway was filled with cars and pick-up trucks, the rolling green lawn crowded with people. And it was familiar. That arch. Then he looked further, toward the house, and his heart stopped beating for just a second.

He stopped the car. Laura sprang from the back seat and Casey from the front, but while Laura ran off into the welcoming arms of a dozen or more people, Casey didn't. She came around to his side of the car, opened the door and gently tugged him out. He didn't argue. He was still staring, standing now beside the car and staring.

That big front porch extended the width of the house, white, with broad steps. The whole thing was lined with silver and gold garland and strings of unlit lights. And there was a porch swing there. Old, but well kept. His throat went tight, and his eyes misted over. In the distorted view now, he could see little Sara, swinging endlessly on the porch swing.

The pain gripped him in iron fists, and he had to tip his head backward in order to breathe, his throat was so tight. He closed his eyes.

"I want to thank you, friend, for lookin' after the Jones girls."

Marcus brought his head down, looked at a man with a star pinned to his shirt. A man with familiar eyes.

"Garrett Brand," he said, thrusting out a hand.

"Good to meet you." Marcus shook but never gave his name. He saw the way Garrett's eyes narrowed on him, searching his face, almost as if he felt the sense of déjà vu, as well, and was trying to identify its cause.

"These little ladies are kinda special to us."

"To me, too," he blurted, then wondered why he'd said it when he was trying so hard not to let them be. "Did Casey explain the situation?"

"Told me about half what I'd have liked her to, but all she could, she said. Stubborn one, that Casey Jones."

"Is she?" Marcus glanced past the big guy, didn't see Casey in the throng of people but noticed instead the horses grazing nearby. Ghosts from the past haunted him again, damn them. For an instant he saw Sara, dark curls bouncing wildly as she sat atop a gentle mare and one of their cousins led her around. He could even hear the faint echo of her sweet laughter. "God, she loved it here," he muttered.

"What's that?"

"Nothing," Marcus said. "I have to go."

He turned to get back into the car, but the memories were still coming. He remembered the oldest of his cousins tugging him away from where he was watching his little sister take her first horseback ride. Saying she'd be fine with the others, that the two of them should go practice bull roping while there was still time.

And that boy—he'd been really big for his age, but gentle. Kind. And his name...it was...

Marcus turned and looked back at Garrett, blinking in shock. My God, it was true.

"I get the oddest feeling we've met before," Garrett said, looking just as puzzled as Marcus knew he himself must.

"I'm not from around here," he said. Then he got into the car, closed the door, started the engine, tried not to hyperventilate.

He managed to keep the car on the road until he was out of sight of the ranch. Then he pulled over, squeezed his head between his hands and bent over the wheel. "How can it be? How the hell can it be?"

"How can what be?"

He went rigid. Sat up fast and straight and glanced up to the rearview mirror, only to meet a pair of sad brown eyes, glittering like jewels from behind damp lashes.

Then she moved, and her hands came to his shoulders, massaging with firm, delicious pressure. "Relax, Marcus. Let go of all this tension. Come on, lean back. That's better."

She forced a sigh from him, made him do as she said with her hypnotic voice and soothing touch.

"What are you doing here, Casey?" he asked her. "You were supposed to stay at the ranch."

"I never said I would, did I?"

No, he realized slowly. She hadn't.

"I don't want to be at the ranch. I want to be with you." She stopped rubbing his shoulders and clambered over the seat, turning around and sitting beside him. "What happened to you back there, Marcus?"

He shook his head. "Nothing."

"Nothing my foot. You acted like you'd been there before. Like it was killing you to be there again. Do you know those people?"

He shook his head. "You knew, didn't you?"

She stared into his eyes, willing him to talk. "I don't know anything, Marcus. But I'd like to."

"Then why did you take me out there?"

She tilted her head. "Do you know them?"

"I don't know, dammit!" He clamped his teeth together in an agonized grimace. "I don't know," he said more softly. "I might have, once..."

"In this childhood you can't remember?"

He nodded, didn't meet her eyes.

She cupped his face in one hand, fingers reaching into his hair. "Don't you want to remember, Marcus?"

"The only thing I want to remember is the name of the man who murdered my family," he told her. "The name my mother screamed before he gunned her down in cold blood."

"But not the good times that came before all that?"

"No."

"Why, Marcus?"

He lifted his head, met her eyes. "Because I lost all that. Remembering only causes pain, Casey. Makes me miss what I had. Makes me want…"

"Want what? To feel that way again? To love again, Marcus? To *be loved* by someone else?"

"That can never happen."

"Don't be too sure about that."

"Don't—"

"Sh…" She leaned close, eyes closed, and gently pressed her lips to his.

So sweet. Softness, every time he looked at her, thought of her, touched her. Comfort. Warmth. She tasted good. He didn't want to, but he kissed her back. A gentle kiss, soothing and healing. His arms around her, hers hugging him close. His mouth moving slowly over hers, while her lips parted and allowed him to feed. His hands in her silken cloud of hair and her breasts pressed to him. She was all softness, every bit of her. Yielding, receptive—like a harbor to a lonely sailor long lost at sea. Like a pool of crystalline water to a man who's just crossed the desert. Like home, waiting to welcome him.

And just when the kiss deepened and heated and started to flare up into something more, something beyond tenderness and healing and softness, she gently pulled away.

Eyes sparkling, she stared into his. A sad little smile curving her lips even as her lashes grew damp, she whispered, "You're like a hurricane, you know that? You show up, and everything inside me gets whipped into a state of chaos.''

He held her gaze, playing idly with a strand of her hair. "I'm not trying to, Casey. I never meant—''

"I know. But that doesn't mean the howl of the wind isn't scaring the hell out of me.''

"I'd never hurt you.''

"Not deliberately. I know that. Still, I don't imagine hurricanes intend to hurt anything. But when they blow away, they leave nothing but rubble behind.''

His gaze lowered, dwelling now on her lips, her mouth. The animal in him wanted to kiss her again. Kiss her deep and hard and long. She wanted him, he knew she did. He could have her right now. If he pulled her against him, if he seduced her, she'd surrender.

She emitted some force, and it pulled at him. He swayed closer.

And stopped himself. Because despite the primitive drives she instigated in him, there was still something of the hero left. The hero he'd always wanted to be, yet never quite measured up to—Caine, the man who'd saved his life and then changed its course utterly. A man of honor.

"A wise woman doesn't stand in the path of the storm, Casey. It would be smarter to stay clear of it. Take cover.''

She sighed, and he knew she was afraid. "Sometimes,'' she whispered, "I just can't go inside. I'm so fascinated by the lightning.''

"Lightning destroys the thing it's attracted to,'' he warned her.

Her lips trembled. "Then you do want me."

"I thought it was fairly obvious."

"A girl likes to be told." Her blush was pretty. Deep pink coloring her cheeks like a slow burn. She was so damned pleased she could barely keep herself from smiling. A gleam of feminine satisfaction lit her eyes.

"Sweet Casey," he told her, and he caught her face between his palms, making her look him in the eyes. "Understand that what you're imagining can never be."

Lowering her lids to half-mast, she hid her eyes from him. "I don't know what you—"

"Yes you do. You're dreaming of promises, Casey. There's forever in your eyes. But what do you see in mine? Hmm? Look, Casey, get rid of all the fairy tales clouding your vision and look at me."

She lifted her gaze, met his eyes head-on.

"I'm looking."

"Then you must see. While you're dreaming of picket fences and rose-covered cottages, I'm dreaming of sex. Hot, sweaty, intensely pleasurable, but utterly meaningless, sex. A night, maybe two, rolling around in each other's arms, followed by a kiss goodbye. No backward glances, no regrets. The one-night stand you said you'd never have. That's what's in my eyes, Casey, and if you can't see it there, you're only kidding yourself."

Every word made her flinch, every sentence brought the shimmering tears closer to the surface. He was pummeling her bloody and his weapons were mere words. The bruises they caused made it pretty obvious she already cared more than she should. He was doing her a favor. But when a teardrop spilled from her eyes onto her cheek, he felt like an assassin.

She said nothing.

What was there to say?

He pulled the car onto the road and pointed it back toward the hotel. And he drove in utter silence for the better part of an hour, while Casey leaned back against the seat with her eyes closed and her cheeks wet. Hands folded tightly in her lap, trembling a little. No sobbing. No hysterics. She had class, Casey Jones did.

But then she spoke, in a voice gone utterly calm and as soft as a whisper. "Those aren't the things I see in your eyes, Marcus."

He closed his eyes briefly, felt a stab of fear spear his heart, tried to ignore it.

"What I see is a boy, deep down inside there, trapped or being held hostage. A boy who is hurting so much he can't bear it. A boy who lost everything he ever loved, and who wants to scream out loud in anguish—but you won't let him. Instead you hide him underneath this facade of a man who doesn't need anyone. You keep him in solitary confinement with your secret identity and your life as Silver City's hero. And you convince yourself he's not even there. But he is, Marcus. I see him. He's the part of you that can love me. And I can reach him and pull him out of that dark hole where you keep him. I can...*I will.*"

Her words fell like hot coals on an old wound. Each one burning away another layer of the veneer he wore and getting closer to the flesh underneath.

Each one bringing fresh, cleansing, stinging air and light and heat to that old wound. And it hurt, God, it hurt so much.

"You're going to get hurt if you let yourself think that way, Casey. I warned you...don't care about me."

"Too late," she whispered.

Twelve

He'd never been scared silent before. He was now. He didn't speak, couldn't speak again until he pulled into the hotel parking lot and reached past Casey to open her door. "Get out. Go straight to the suite and stay there with Graham until you hear from me."

She didn't move. "And where will you be?"

"Your place."

"Why?" She was staring at him. Marcus managed to remain looking straight ahead. He didn't want to look into those knowing eyes. Not now. But he could feel them on him, hunting, searching for something that she'd never find. "You have a plan, don't you?"

"If you want to call it a plan," he said. "Your sister's assailant will probably try again tonight. When he does, I'll be there waiting."

"And then what?"

"And then I make him tell me what's going on and turn him over to the police. It'll be over."

"And you'll be gone."

He lowered his head, because her words sent a searing pain through his chest that had no business being there. "That's right."

She reached out, gripped the door and pulled it closed. "I'm going with you."

He only shook his head.

"He's not an idiot, Marcus. He'll be watching. He'll know you came back alone—that it's a trap. But if he sees me, he might—"

"Might what? Think you're Laura? Grab you instead of her?" He reached past her and opened the door once again. "Leave the crime fighting to me, okay, Casey? I know what I'm doing."

"I really doubt that." But this time, she got out.

Marcus was pulling away even as she shoved the door closed.

She was infuriating. And how the hell was he supposed to think, to plan, when she kept him so distracted he could barely remember his own name?

He wanted her. He told himself that was all. Physical desire and nothing more. But somewhere inside he knew that was a lie.

Casey didn't go straight to the suite and doubted Graham even realized they'd returned. Taking a quick, precautionary glance around the parking lot, she determined that Graham wasn't lurking out here somewhere, watching her. There were only cars parked in neat rows. Mostly empty. A man sat in one. She could only see the shape of his head, dimly silhouetted in the shadowy interior. The car was running. But he definitely wasn't Graham. Too big.

Taking a breath, she went to the spot where she'd parked her car and opened the door.

Then she went still.

What was she doing? Running after Marcus like some love-struck, desperate wimp? No. No, he cared for her, dammit, and he was going to realize that sooner or later. Let him sleep on it tonight. Alone. Let him think about what could have happened if he'd taken her with him. Let him dream about making love to her...and wake up sweating and wishing she was there. Chasing him wasn't going to help. Giving in to her burning desire for him, telling him a one-night stand was enough after all, that would do no good, either.

Let him sweat it out tonight. And maybe tomorrow...

She slammed the door and spun toward the hotel before she could change her mind.

The explosion came from nowhere...and everywhere. A roar that pierced her eardrums and then her brain. A force that slammed into her, searing hot and so powerful her body rocketed forward. She hit the pavement hard, felt the impact, the burn of her flesh being scraped away as she skidded over the blacktop. Pain screamed from so many locations she couldn't pinpoint one. An all-over pain—as if her entire body were on fire. Dizziness swamped her, blurred her vision as she weakly lifted her head, wondering what the hell had happened.

In the distance, the man got out of his car and stood looking toward her for just a second. His form swam as she blinked, trying to clear her vision. And for a moment, she brought him into focus. And she knew.

The bastard who'd tried to hurt Laura.

He gave a satisfied nod and got into his car. Casey strained to see it, to form a mental photograph of it in her mind. She squinted at the plates as the black smoke rose to distort her vision once again.

Or maybe it wasn't smoke at all, because that blackness seemed to close in all around her, and a second later, it was all there was.

Marcus had gone maybe a block when he heard the explosion. It seemed to reverberate right through him, and he knew...

"Jesus, no..."

Yanking the wheel to the left, he pulled a squealing U-turn. Cars skidded, horns blasted. Marcus stamped the accelerator, took a corner on two wheels and came to a screeching halt in the hotel lot. Red-orange flames, thick black smoke, people running around like ants on amphetamines. And Casey, lying very still, facedown on the ground, thin wisps of smoke trailing skyward from her clothes.

Marcus lunged from the car and ran toward her, shoving his way through the crowd gathered to gawk at her. "Get an ambulance, dammit!" He didn't hear the reply, couldn't hear a thing because his heart was hammering so loudly in his ears. He fell to his knees beside her and, careful not to move her, tore the smoldering blouse down its center and pulled it away from her skin. His hands shook when he lifted her hair away from her neck and pressed his fingers to her throat, praying silently that he would feel an answering beat.

There. She was alive.

"Casey. Casey, can you hear me?"

No reply. Moving her hair away from her face, he

touched her cheek. Then patted it gently. "Casey, wake up. Talk to me, come on."

Sirens screamed in the distance, growing louder. Someone yelled, "Let me through, I'm a doctor."

Casey's eyes fluttered open. She tried to lift her head.

"Don't move. Lie still, Casey. Just lie still."

"It hurts…" A bare whisper. Pain in her eyes.

"I know. Hold on, help is on the way."

Her eyes closed in pain. Her breath came in stutters, ragged, uneven. Sucked through her clenched teeth.

"Don't close your eyes. Don't, Casey…"

"Let me in here," someone said. A man with a bag. The doctor, Marcus figured. He started to move, to get out of the way. But Casey's hand suddenly gripped his with a strength that surprised him.

"Don't leave me…."

His breath caught in his throat. "I'm not gonna leave you. I'm right here."

The ambulance arrived. Paramedics shoved him aside, and her hand was pulled from his. They surrounded her, blocking his view of her as he got to his feet and staggered a few steps backward. His knees felt like water, his stomach like a vat filled with boiling acid.

"Marcus…?" She said it softly, brokenly. His name, over and over. "Marcus?"

"I'm right here."

"Pressure is dropping," someone said.

"Could be internal injuries," another replied.

Marcus's head swam. He had to brace himself on

the hood of a nearby car to keep from losing his balance, and for the first time in his life he thought he might actually pass out cold.

"Get that backboard over here! Move!"

"Pressure's still falling."

He couldn't see what they were doing, couldn't get close enough. "Don't let her die," he told them. "Damn you, don't let her die."

A hand fell on his shoulder, and Marcus turned. Graham stood beside him, grim-faced, pale. "It's futile, isn't it?"

"Don't even think that. She's going to be all right. She has to be."

"Oh, I agree. But what I meant, Marcus, was the futility of trying not to care. It's not possible, you know. And losing someone hurts just as much when you haven't admitted it, to them or to yourself. Maybe even a little more, wouldn't you say?"

They lowered the backboard beside Casey, and several men gripped her body, her head, her shoulders. They counted and carefully turned her over, so she lay faceup on the board. And then they strapped her to it. Strapped her head down. Her eyes were closed, her face ashen. When they lifted the board and moved toward the ambulance, Marcus was right behind them.

"The police are on the way, sir," one of the medics told him. A short blond man lugging a heavy-looking case. "They'll want to talk to you."

"Then they'd best come to the hospital, because that's where I'll be."

The younger man met Marcus's gaze and didn't argue. "You can follow us. I'd let you in the back, but we need to be back there, for her sake, and there's only so much room."

With a brief nod, he conceded the point.

"She your wife?"

The question startled him, and he looked down sharply.

The medic shrugged. "It's kind of obvious. You look like you're the one who got blown across the parking lot. Hey, maybe you should have someone drive you..."

The ambulance door opened, and they lifted her inside. "I can drive," Marcus muttered. The medics clambered in beside her. The door closed, and the sound seemed abnormally loud. Final. Like a gunshot.

"We're gonna take good care of her," the kid said, and he shoved the bag into a compartment on the side of the vehicle before climbing into the front.

"You'd damned well better," Marcus said, but no one heard. The ambulance was already pulling away, siren bawling, lights flashing.

"The lad was right," Graham said. "I'll drive you to the hospital."

Chin falling to his chest, Marcus didn't argue. He walked to the car, got in the passenger side, let Graham take the wheel. Graham pulled out into traffic and passed three vehicles in a no-passing lane, jerking the car back to the right about a half second before an oncoming delivery truck would have hit him. Then he ran a red light with the skill of Mario Andretti.

Marcus, who'd come to full attention during the unexpected maneuvers, turned to stare at the older man. "I didn't know you could drive like that."

"There's a lot you don't know, Marcus. Some of it far more important than the extent of my…skills."

"What don't I know about?"

"Life, my friend. Life."

Sighing, Marcus mustered patience. "This isn't the time for subtle lectures, Graham."

"Then I suppose you'll be asking what I found when I searched the Jones house."

Marcus pinched the bridge of his nose between thumb and forefinger, closed his eyes tight. "I don't even care."

"That's good, because I didn't do it."

His head came up slowly. "You what?"

"I didn't search the house." He passed a semi on the wrong side of the road, making use of the sidewalk without ever once blinking an eye.

"Why the hell not?"

"Because it was the wrong thing to do. It would have been a mistake. And…it was rather unethical."

"Unethical? *Unethical?* Correct me if I'm wrong, Graham, but didn't you used to work for the CIA?"

Graham only smiled. "How old do you think I am, Marcus?"

"I don't know. Fifty-something?"

"I was fifty-something before Caine died."

Marcus blinked, searched the man's craggy face. He never seemed to age.

"I've been around a good deal longer than you have, Marcus. And I'd like to think I've learned a few things." He zipped around a bus and emerged right behind the ambulance.

"Like how to drive?"

"Like what's important."

"And I suppose you're going to tell me what's important."

"That girl up there. Her sister. And today. What's not important is the past. It's as gone as if it never existed."

"Not to me, it's not."

"Maybe not. Maybe it can't be. But you have to ask yourself if the past is important enough to let it rob you of a future."

"I have a future. As The Guardian."

"It's no future at all."

"It was good enough for Caine."

"And Caine died a lonely, unfulfilled man. All he had, all he ever had in the world was you. For him it was enough. But what if you hadn't come along?"

Frowning, Marcus turned away.

"He'd have had an aging houseman, an empty mansion and a pile of money. Is that going to be enough for you, Marcus? It's something you need to decide now, before it's too late. It wasn't enough for Caine. Nor for the Guardian before him. They both lived to have regrets I hope you'll never have."

The ambulance pulled into the hospital lot, and Graham pulled in, as well. Opening the door, Marcus got out and stood frozen as they wheeled Casey in through the automatic doors.

"Think about it, Marcus," Graham said. Then he leaned over, closed the car door and drove away.

"As if I could do anything *but* think about it," Marcus said. His throat was dry, his hands damp as he hurried into the hospital.

* * *

"Marcus?"

"Right here, Casey. Right here."

A large hand closed around hers as Casey opened her eyes and battled the disoriented confusion swimming in her brain. She'd been sleeping, but felt scared. She'd been aching, but didn't know why.

"Where are we? What's—" Her eyes finally found his, and when they did she went silent. He looked so…stricken. White, with worry lines around his eyes that had never been there before. His lips were tight, thin.

"You're okay." His hand on hers tightened, a reassuring squeeze. "Bruised up pretty well, and there are some burns on your back, but…"

"The car…" She felt her stomach twist as she recalled what had happened. The explosion. The pain. The stranger.

"Looks like it was a bomb," Marcus said softly. "The bastard rigged it to go off when the driver's door was opened and closed again. He probably hoped to take you both out."

She blinked, searching her mind. There was something…she had to tell him. Something she'd told herself not to forget.

"Thank God it didn't work. What the hell were you doing, Casey? I told you to go straight to the suite. Why did you—"

"You know why."

His dark gaze held hers for a long, tense moment. "You were coming to the house. To help me nail the bad guys like some kind of supergirl, right, Casey?"

"If you can be Batman, I can be Wonder Woman," she said softly. "But that's not why I was coming."

He looked at her, lifted his brows. "Why, then?"

"To be with you."

Slowly, he lowered his head. "I already told you—"

"It can't happen. I know. And don't run screaming yet, Marcus. I changed my mind. That's why I didn't get into the car. Instead I slammed the door and turned away, and that's when…" She closed her eyes. "I wasn't going to tell you any of that."

"Must be the pain medication."

She met his gaze once more. "So all I had to do to get you back was get myself blown up, huh? Maybe I should make a note…for future reference."

"I'd rather you try some less traumatic method next time."

"Are you saying there will be a next time, then?"

He looked away.

"I didn't think so." She sighed, tried to sit up, winced a little when the sheets rubbed across a sore spot on her back. "There was something else, something…someone…" She bit her lip, and it came back to her. "He was there. I saw him."

Dark brows drew together until they nearly touched. "The—"

"Yes. Yes, get a pen, Marcus." Closing her eyes, she dragged the reluctant memory to the surface and fought to keep it there. "Silver car…. Mercedes, it was a Mercedes. Texas plates. K…S…G. Yes, it was G. Seven-six-nine."

Once it was out, she felt safe to open her eyes

again, only to see Marcus scribbling the information down on a pad. When he looked up, there was admiration in his gaze. "How did you possibly—"

"I noticed him there just before...and then when I looked up, he was standing there, just looking at me. I took a long look at that Mercedes before I passed out."

He shook his head slowly, then leaned over and stroked her hair. "You're something else, Casey Jones. Must be one hell of a reporter."

"I am."

He nodded at that. "Are you hurting?"

"Not unbearably."

"They want to keep you overnight. The doctor thought there were internal injuries at first, when your blood pressure started falling like a stone. You scared the hell out of me, Casey."

"Good."

He sent her a quizzical frown, then went on. "Turns out it was only shock. You're okay. And...I can't let you stay the night here."

She thought for a moment, then nodded. "It's exactly where he'd expect to find me, once he realizes I survived the blast."

"Right. And you're far too vulnerable here. I want you home, where I can protect you. You think you're up to that?"

"Gee, I don't know. Let me think on this a minute. I can either spend the night with a bunch of nurses, or I can spend it with my own personal superman. What a decision."

"Casey—"

His voice held a warning tone, and she knew he was about to tell her not to keep hoping, not to keep wanting him, to stop flirting so shamelessly.

She turned her hand in his, linked their fingers and said, "Shut up and take me home, Marcus."

He nodded. "I'll tell them to get your release forms in order. I've been fending off cops all afternoon, by the way, but I think I've finally got them convinced neither of us has a clue why anyone would want to ransack your house or blow you to bits. They'll leave us alone...for a while, at least."

"Thanks. I don't want to deal with them right now. Hell, they'll be questioning every lowlife I ever exposed in print—and half the ones I'm investigating."

"I hadn't even thought of that. Just that they'd get in the way of my catching this bastard." Marcus pulled a phone from his pocket, thumbing the buttons. "Graham, I have a plate I want you to run for me. Ready?"

He read off the plate number, along with the description of the car, and as he did, he paced. When he finished the call and dropped the phone into his pocket, he turned to go. But just then the door opened and a nurse came walking in. Casey was so startled by the intrusion that she emitted a squeak of alarm. And as soon as she did, Marcus's eyes were on her again, concerned.

"Nurse, can you have someone get Ms. Jones's release forms ready and have them brought in here?"

"But she shouldn't be leaving—"

"She's leaving." Marcus came closer, sat down on the edge of the bed. "And until she does, I'm not. So if there's a problem with that, we'd better address it now.''

He spoke to the nurse, but his eyes were on Casey. Silently reassuring her that he wasn't going anywhere. That he wouldn't leave her vulnerable to another attempt by this maniac who'd turned all their lives upside down.

It was in that instant that she knew she loved him.

Her breath came a little faster, she felt her pulse rate quicken. Damn, she hadn't meant to fall…not this far, this fast. It was a risk. She wasn't sure if it was a wise risk…or one she was willing to take.

But it didn't really matter, anyway. She no longer had a choice.

''Just so you know, this is against my better judgment.'' He stood beside the car, holding the passenger door open for her as Casey got out.

''As long as you're sure there's not a bomb waiting for us inside…''

''I doubt it.''

''Try not to be so reassuring.'' She put her feet on the blacktop of her driveway, started to stand, then grimaced.

''Hurts, huh?'' He leaned over, pulled one of her arms around his shoulders and helped her to her feet.

''Getting blown up does that to me.'' She winced when he started to walk her forward.

Marcus knew he shouldn't—because of his own reactions and, from the look of things, hers, as well—but he did it anyway. Turning toward her, he scooped her into his arms and started up the walk.

Casey sighed softly. Her breath caressed his cheek. "A girl could get used to this kind of thing."

"A girl could dig her keys out of her pocket," he said. Flippant, yes. But safe. Unlike the press of her body to his, or the warmth of it suffusing his own.

She wriggled a little, then shook the keys at him. He held her close enough to the door so she could unlock it, and between the two of them they got it open. Marcus carried her inside, paused just past the door to take a look around. Listened, trying to sense any other presence. Nothing seemed out of place. No sixth sense told him anyone had been here.

"I think it's safe," she said. "If we were going to explode, we'd have done it by now, don't you think?"

"Speak for yourself."

She looked up quickly. "Should I take that as a compliment?"

"Forget I said it." He strode across the living room's carpet and lowered her to the sofa. "How you feeling?"

"The burns hurt a little. Walking around isn't too comfy—I imagine because of the scrapes and bruises on my legs. But as long as I'm sitting still, I'm pretty much okay."

"Then stay sitting still."

She made a face. "Sure. You can wait on me all night."

He sketched an exaggerated bow, then straightened again. "Right after I take a look around."

"Be my guest."

"I'll only be a minute."

She smiled, a sly, secret smile he didn't like, because it sent his blood pressure through the roof. "Good."

Marcus swallowed, but it still felt as if his throat were coated in sand. Rather than try to spar with her verbally—tough when a man was rendered speechless so often—he set off to check out the house. Upstairs and down. Inside and out. At last he'd assured himself that no one had been around or tampered with anything. And he didn't see anyone watching, either. Probably their terrorist needed time to regroup.

Or else he was working on getting to her in the hospital. The staff were deliberately keeping Casey's name quiet, so the creep would have no definite proof of which sister he'd nearly killed today.

He peered in at Casey, just to see that she was okay. She lay still on the sofa, eyes closed, looking like his fondest fantasy with her hair spread around her, lips slightly parted, breasts rising and falling with every gentle breath.

Not a good idea to look at her too long, he decided, and ducked back into the kitchen. He rummaged in the fridge, found the makings for a light dinner and started whipping stuff together. A chicken stir-fry was sizzling in no time.

"What's that heavenly smell?" she called.

He poked his head around. "I thought you were sleeping."

"Resting my eyes. And starving. You never told me you could cook."

"I never told you a lot of things."

"Think you ever will?"

MAGGIE SHAYNE 205

He stood silent in the doorway. She sat up slowly and stared at him over the back of the couch. His throat dry, stomach churning, he shrugged. "Depends. What do you want to know?"

"What do I want to know?" She shrugged, and he could see the wheels turning behind her eyes. It scared the hell out of him.

Thirteen

Casey watched him walk into the living room, a plate of food in each hand. He set them down, and she watched him walk out again. She could, she figured, while away a lot of time watching him. He moved like an athlete. Like a dancer. And he probably wasn't even aware of it.

He came back again, bearing drinks this time. Fragrant hot chocolate, steaming and frothy. But her gaze was more interested in the way his hands cupped the mugs, curling around the warm ceramic. Never spilling a drop. He'd asked her what she wanted to know about him. But she thought she knew him well enough by now to realize he wouldn't reveal a bit more than he wanted to.

She sat up a little straighter on the sofa, making room for him to sit beside her, then leaned forward and inhaled the delicious aromas. "Where did you learn to cook like this?"

"Graham. He's rather a jack-of-all-trades."

"Is he?" She tasted a bite of the chicken and vegetables, closed her eyes in pleasure. "How long have you two known each other?"

"Most of my life. You like the chicken?"

She tilted her head to one side. "The chicken is

fabulous. Are my questions making you uncomfortable?''

His lips quirked slightly at the corners. ''You're too perceptive for your own good.''

''I thought so. I was trying not to ask anything too personal.''

''And skating around what you really want to know.''

''You'd rather I come straight to the point?''

He nodded but didn't look her in the eyes. ''I'm not sure you have to. I can guess what you really want to ask about.''

''And if I did ask you about that night...the night that's still giving you bad dreams...would you tell me?''

He shrugged. ''For a long time I could barely remember it. It's funny. Since I've been here, it's been...coming back to me.''

She set her plate aside. ''Do you have any idea why?''

He only shook his head, pushed his food around a little, then set the fork down.

''I made you lose your appetite.''

''No, not you. The memories. It's not a pretty story, Casey. You sure you want to hear it?''

''I'm sure.''

He nodded, licked his lips, lowered his eyes. ''It was three days before Christmas. But I didn't celebrate Christmas that year. I haven't since.''

''Maybe you should.''

He shook his head. ''My father was an accountant, but he was never happy doing taxes and books for a few dollars here and there. He was always looking for a fast buck, always coming up with one easy money scheme or another. You know the type.''

When he looked at her, Casey nodded. But she didn't speak, half-afraid that if she interrupted him now, he'd stop. This was obviously difficult for him.

''He got involved with some of the lowest life-forms on the planet.''

''Criminals?''

He met her eyes, nodded once. ''Money laundering. I didn't know it at the time, but I'm sure that's what it was. He got greedy, started skimming from the clients. One of them caught on.''

Casey closed her eyes slowly.

''Dad came home early that day, and he was scared. I could see it in his face, plain as day.'' Marcus's jaw was tight, his face pinched, tormented. ''He told Mom to go find Sara. She was playing her favorite game of hide-and-seek. She loved that game....'' Lifting his head, he swallowed hard.

Casey put a hand on his cheek. ''You loved her a lot, didn't you.''

''I adored the kid.''

Tears burned in the back of her eyes, but she didn't dare let them spill over.

''Dad said we had to leave right away. He sent me to the basement for the suitcases. While I was down there, someone kicked in the door. Then there was gunfire.''

''Oh, God,'' Casey whispered.

Marcus's hands clasped tight between his knees, and his head hung low. ''I couldn't move. I just froze there, paralyzed. My mother screamed…a name, I think, but I've never been able to remember what it was." He drew a shuddering breath. "After a while there was no more noise. Nothing, just this deathly silence. Not a normal kind of quiet, you know. It was heavy. Different. You could feel it, weighing down on you, smothering you."

She stroked his hair, wishing she could stroke the pain away. Knowing she couldn't.

"When I finally went back up there…they were gone."

"All of them?"

He nodded. "Even at ten, I knew they were dead. The place was ripped apart from the gunfire. There was…blood. Everywhere."

Pressing her hands to her mouth, she stifled a sob, but he heard it, looked up at her. "Don't cry for me, Casey. It was a long time ago."

"That doesn't make it any less heartbreaking." She slid closer to him, put her arms around his waist and lowered her head to his shoulder. "What did you do, Marcus? How did you survive?"

He didn't pull away from her. She heard his sigh. "A man found me wandering around in shock. He took me in, raised me as his own."

She lifted her head to stare into his eyes. "The authorities let him adopt you?"

"As far as the authorities were concerned, I was dead, along with the rest of my family."

"But—"

"If the killer had known where to find me, Casey, he'd have come after me, too. He wouldn't have left any witnesses if he'd had a choice. I figure the only reason he left when he did was because he knew the police were on the way. Otherwise he'd have searched the house. He'd have found me."

"Thank God he didn't." She squeezed him tighter.

Marcus extracted himself very gently. "That man, the one who took me in, was the Guardian. He trained me all my life to take up the role when he could no longer fill it. And when he died, that's what I did."

Casey nodded slowly. "Was he...the first?"

Marcus shook his head. "No, there was another before him. Lately, I've been suspecting the first Guardian might have been someone I know very well." Casey tilted her head, but he said no more on that subject. "There's a reason I'm telling you all of this."

Blinking slowly to dry her eyes, she nodded. "I figured there probably was."

"It's so you'll understand, Casey. So you'll know. All the love I had to give died with my family. The only love left is love for what I do. It's all I have— all I need."

She swallowed hard. So he had finally confided in her just to drive his point home. To make her give up any hope of having something with him. "You only wish that were true. But it isn't, Marcus."

"Isn't it?"

She shook her head. "You still love *them,* don't you?"

The pain that welled up in his dark eyes almost did her in. He averted them, got up and began clearing the plates away. "You should get some sleep," he told her.

"I'll never sleep tonight."

"Try. You've had a hell of a day."

"So have you."

"I'm not the one who got blown across a parking lot."

"No," she said. "But it shook you, didn't it, Marcus?"

He nodded. "I'd hate like hell to see anything happen to you."

"I know." Her eyes held his for the longest time, and she could see the flames leaping to life in them. She got to her feet. But sleep was the last thing on her mind.

He should have been worried when Casey went upstairs with no more than a token argument. Especially after that blazing-hot parting glance. But he wasn't exactly clearheaded and analytical. He wasn't sure what made him tell her his deepest secrets. Oh, he'd told himself that knowing the truth would put a damper on her feelings for him—would convince her once and for all that he was incapable of returning those feelings.

It hadn't worked. That much was obvious. But talking to her had been cathartic for him. He'd never done it, relived that day out loud to another living soul. It felt as if a huge weight had been lifted from him. As if just getting it out had somehow eased the burden.

And he wanted her more now than he ever had.

Soft footsteps made him turn. Then his throat went dry.

She stood at the foot of the stairs, and for a second he thought he was dreaming. She wore a white nightgown, as sheer as a breeze. Her flesh beneath it was perfectly visible, and he caught glimpses of rose and peach, curves and silken curls. Her hair tumbled down around her shoulders, and her eyes were wide and hungry.

She looked like an angel...a dangerous angel.

He could only stare as she came closer. Lick his lips, try to clear his throat.

"Casey..."

"Don't talk. Don't think, either. Not about the past...or the future. Nothing, Marcus. Nothing but tonight." She stopped, standing close to him, and slowly slipped her hands up the front of his shirt. Warm fingers on his flesh, gentle pressure. Insistence. She wouldn't be denied.

His heart pounded in reaction to her simple touch. "I can't love you, Casey." It sounded more like a plea than a statement of fact.

"But I can love you," she whispered. "Let me, Marcus. Let me love you tonight."

Standing on tiptoe, she pressed her mouth to his. He shivered but didn't resist her. He didn't *want* to resist her. He needed this, craved it. And he gently slipped his arms around her waist, careful not to hurt her. Pulling her close, bowing over her, he kissed her deeply.

Her lips parted, eager, inviting. So soft. Marcus tasted her mouth with his tongue, and she tipped her head back farther, sighing softly. He buried his hands in her hair, held her head to him as he fed from her mouth. His hips arched against her, and she returned the pressure.

When he broke the kiss, her eyes fluttered open, and he saw the need in them. Hot and desperate, it matched his own. He ran his hands down the slender column of her neck to her shoulders. She stood motionless as he drew his hands lower, covering her breasts, and she sucked in a sudden gasp and let her head fall backward. Squeezing, kneading her, he closed his fingers on her nipples and felt them harden as he applied pressure. She made a pleading sound in her throat, so he pinched harder.

Then he took his hands away. They were shaking. She met his eyes.

"Take it off." His voice was hoarse, a bare whisper.

She stood in front of him, only a step away, and lifted the nightgown over her head, then dropped it to the floor. She stood there, naked, vulnerable. But bold, uninhibited. She didn't cringe or try to hide. She stood and let him devour her body with his eyes. He could barely draw a breath as he looked at her perfect breasts, her pale skin, her waist, her thighs and the haven between them. Even her bruised, scraped knees were beautiful to him.

"I...you're...incredible," he told her.

His hands shook when he reached for her again. He cupped her breasts, naked to him now, lifted them and bent to feed, to suckle and nip and tug at their tender crests. Casey shuddered, gasped, but stood for him. As if she'd let him do anything he liked tonight. As if she only sought his pleasure. But it was hers he wanted to see…to feel.

He pulled her close, kissed her and gently tumbled to the floor without letting go.

She landed on top of him, her hands working the buttons of his shirt free, pushing it away from his chest. Then running slowly over his skin. She pressed her mouth to his chest and muttered that he was the most beautiful man she'd ever known. When her teeth grazed his nipple, he jolted in pleasure. Then her lips trailed lower, over his belly, and she undid his jeans and pushed them away, too. And then she mouthed him, and he clung to her and gasped for air.

Could he die of passion? Was it possible?

She slithered up his body once more, settled herself over him, sheathed him inside her, expelling all her breath at once. Marcus closed his hands on her hips to pull her closer, push himself deeper. Her head tipped backward, and she began to move. A fleeting embrace, a dancing rhythm. He felt more than passion now. This wasn't something so simple as that. It was more. It was deeper. It was psychic—a soul kiss. She seemed to read him, to know what he needed even before he did. She moved, caressed, kissed him, slowed her pace and quickened it by some uncanny instinct. She pulled him like a magnet, drawing something from the center of him, the core. Pulling it into her soft body and cradling it there like something precious.

He responded by touching her, the pressure of his thumbs at the place where they were joined, circling, rubbing, knowing each time she shivered that he was doing it right. He caught one breast in his mouth and held to it. When she reached the brink of madness he knew, because she pulled him over the edge, and he tumbled with her into a quagmire of sensation. He could have drowned in feeling. In release. In... emotion. In pumping the very essence of himself into her, and feeling her body grip and pull in search of more.

She screamed his name and then went limp, her body collapsing atop his and going still.

His arms were around her waist, holding her gently. Her hair tickled his face, and her body was soft upon his. He felt enveloped in warmth, safety—utterly protected from the darkness in his soul, the darkness where he'd lived for so long. From the past. From the pain.

He stroked her hair. He had thought she looked like an angel. Now he wondered if that was more accurate than he could have imagined. He'd never felt so light. So...complete.

Or so bewildered.

He should say something, he realized. She was lying atop him, still, waiting. Wondering, maybe, what he was thinking. He should say...something. But what?

"Casey?"

She didn't answer.

Marcus gently pushed her hair away from her face and tipped his head up. Her eyes were closed, her breath coming evenly, slowly. She was asleep.

And her cheeks were damp.

Marcus's stomach tightened. But he didn't move, didn't want to wake her. Instead he reached the blanket on the sofa and pulled it over her. And he lay there beneath a sleeping, weeping angel. All night.

Laura's stalker never showed. In the morning, Casey stirred, looked down into his eyes, smiled a little self-consciously.

He touched a bruise on her cheek. It had been red and slightly puffy last night. Now it was pale blue and purple. "Does it hurt?"

"Nothing could hurt today," she told him.

He looked away. "Last night—"

"Didn't mean anything?" She touched his chin, turning him to face her. "I was here, remember?"

"Casey—"

"It meant something to me. That's enough for now. It's not like you didn't warn me. So…what's for breakfast?"

"I don't want to hurt you," he told her.

"I'm a big girl, Marcus. Let me worry about myself, okay?"

He only shook his head. He never should have given in to the temptation last night. She was going to be hurt when he left, there was no getting around that. He could have kicked himself.

"So, you cooking or what?"

"It's your turn," he told her, trying to keep the grim certainty from his voice.

"Okay, cold cereal it is. Right after I call the Brand ranch to check in on my sister. If the phone is working, that is."

"That's not a good idea. Suppose the phone's bugged."

She frowned at him. About that time the telephone rang, and she damn near jumped out of her luscious skin. He reached for it as she got up and wrapped herself in the blanket, leaving him utterly naked on the floor.

"How is Ms. Jones this morning?" Graham asked.

"Better. Almost as good as new, in fact. What have you got for me, Graham?"

"Straight to the point as always. And I can't tell a thing from your voice."

"That's because it's none of your business."

Graham cleared his throat. "That tells me all I wanted to know," he said. "I finished the trace on the plate number you gave me. It's a rental. A man calling himself Remington signed for it, paid cash."

Marcus nodded. "Remington. Is that an alias?"

"Yes, but fortunately a known one. A.K. Remington is one of several aliases used by one of the Silver City underworld's most notorious players. He's spent the last twenty years in prison on a racketeering conviction, but he's guilty of far worse things. There's just never been any proof. His other names are Alexander James Mancini, AJ Mancini, Captain Mancini—seems he liked to use his old Air Force title as often as—"

"Captain Mancini...." Marcus's grip on the phone faltered. His knees shook. In his mind, he heard it again. His mother's final scream, her choked, terrified voice. *No, Captain Mancini. No...please...don't....*

And then the rat-a-tat of the automatic weapon…the dull thud of bullets ripping into flesh. The soft sound of his mother's body sinking to the floor. The smells of blood and sulfur and hot lead.

The phone hit the floor hard. Graham's tinny voice shouted his name from the receiver, but Marcus only stood there.

"Marcus?" Casey came to him, touched him, searched his face. Then she picked up the phone. "Graham?"

"Is everything all right, dear?"

"Yes, I think so. He'll…he'll call you back, okay?" She hung up the phone, anchored the blanket underneath her arms and gripped Marcus's shoulders. "Talk to me, Marcus. What is it?"

Swallowing hard, he closed his eyes against the memory. Pressed his palms to the sides of his head. "The car you saw…"

"Yes?"

Slowly, he opened his eyes, his head spinning as he faced her. "It belongs to the man who murdered my family twenty-two years ago, Casey."

She blinked, opened her mouth, closed it again.

"The name…I remember the name my mother screamed. It's the same name—"

"Okay. Okay, let's just think this through. It makes no sense, you realize that. So…so maybe—"

"How many mobsters named Captain Mancini do you suppose there are?"

Casey shook her head. "But, Marcus, why would that same man be after my sister? What in the world could—"

"I don't know. I just…I don't…"

"All right. All right, just take it slow. We'll figure it out, Marcus. We'll get to the bottom of this... together. Okay?"

He closed his eyes, nodded. But no matter what she did or said, he couldn't get the sound of his mother's voice to stop ringing in his ears.

"I'm going to get that son of a bitch, Casey. I'm going to kill him for what he did."

"I know," she whispered. "I know."

Fourteen

Casey had a gut feeling. She never ignored her gut feelings, but this one wasn't full-blown just yet. Or maybe it was, and she was choosing not to see it.

But it was right there, like a name you couldn't quite remember hovering on the tip of your tongue. She couldn't grab hold of it, couldn't touch it or identify it. But it was there, gnawing at her soul and scaring the hell out of her for some reason.

She had to talk to Laura. Now.

"I need to go into the office, Marcus," she told him later that afternoon, after she'd spent too much time pacing and worrying. "Just for an hour. Will you be okay?"

He stared at her for a long moment. "What's going on, Casey?"

"Nothing." She said it too quickly. Saw the suspicion in his eyes. God, he still didn't trust her, not fully, even after last night and the things she'd said to him. The feelings he'd shared. "I just...want to get out of here for a little while, and I have some work there. The drive will do me good. I'll bring the work home. To distract me. This waiting for some bastard to show up and take a shot at us is driving me nuts."

He nodded. "You're forgetting, you don't have a car."

She pursed her lips. "I could take yours…?"

Looking slightly more at ease, but still wary, he tossed her the keys. "I'll check under the hood first."

"I wouldn't leave if you didn't."

His sigh was heavy. Final. As if he sensed somehow that there was something she was keeping from him.

She'd tell him, once she knew herself for sure. It was only the barest kernel of a hunch, one she couldn't even put her finger on just yet. "I'll be back soon."

"Be careful, Casey."

She was up to something. He knew it, but he wasn't sure what, and he figured the only way he'd ever know would be to give her enough rope to hang herself. He had a feeling that whatever her plan was, it would blow up in his face soon enough.

"Who are you kidding?"

He went very still, surprised at the words coming from his own lips. Talking to himself was not a habit of his, no matter how solitary his life-style.

Was he kidding himself? Looking for any excuse to distrust her, to suspect her? Maybe because that way it would be easier to deny his…

His what? His feelings for her? But he didn't *have* any feelings for her.

He watched her go, closed his eyes. "She's up to something. I know it, and since when did I let a pretty face make me doubt my own instincts?"

Closing the door, he turned to face the empty house. He had yet to take a thorough look around the place. He'd asked Graham to do so, but Graham had let him down. For the first time ever.

And maybe that should tell you something, Marcus.

No. There was no reason to treat this case any differently than any other. He stepped forward and started looking. And he wasn't even certain what for.

She didn't use her office phone. Instead, she used one in a co-worker's office, keeping Marcus's words about bugs in mind.

One of the countless Brands answered on the third ring. Casey heard Christmas music coming from a radio, drowned out by the chatter of voices, all of them happy.

God, Laura must be hating it there.

Finally, her sister's voice came on the phone. And Casey didn't waste any time with preamble.

"Do you love me, Laura?"

There was a brief moment of silence on the other end. "Well, what kind of a question is that? You know I do."

Nodding, Casey twisted the phone cord around her finger, untwisted it again. "I need you to tell me what happened to you before you came to us, Laura."

"Casey, I—"

"No. No, this is important. This involves me now, and it looks like Marcus is all wrapped up in it, too." She bit her lip. "Laura, I've never asked you for anything as important to me as this is. Please…"

"What's going on with you, Casey? What—has something happened? Between you and Marcus?"

"Besides my falling head over heels in love with him, you mean?"

"Oh, Casey…"

"I know. Stupid, hopeless and self-destructive. I know."

There was another silence. Then Laura said, "I like him. He fits in our little family, you know? It feels like he's a part of it already."

"We'll have a hard time convincing him of that."

"I sort of got that feeling. He's a real loner, isn't he, Case?"

"I'm working on that. Meanwhile, I need to know—"

"If I tell you, you end up being a target. It's because I love you so much that I can't—"

"I'm already a target."

Laura gasped. "What are you saying? Casey, has something happened? Are you okay?"

"I'm fine. The bastard put a bomb in my car, but I wasn't in it when it went off."

"Oh, my God!"

"So you see, nothing you tell me can make matters any worse. There's nothing to lose. Talk to me, Laura. For the love of God, if you ever cared about me, talk to me now."

"This is my fault. It's all my fault, Casey. And to think I've brought all this down on you—"

"Dammit, Laura, tell me!"

Laura went silent, stunned perhaps. Casey had never raised her voice to her sister before. "Okay," she whispered. "Okay. I'll tell you what I know. But it isn't much."

"What do you mean, it isn't much?"

"I was four years old, Casey. I don't remember. Hell, I only know that…that my family was murdered, and that I was there when it happened."

Casey whispered an expletive. Her mouth went dry and her eyes wide. Every cell in her body tuned in to her sister's words. "What else?"

"Nothing. The police found me hiding in a kitchen cabinet. They put me into the witness protection program. They felt that if the killer could find me, I'd be in danger. That he'd probably believe I could identify him and try to get rid of me."

"And could you?"

Laura sighed heavily into the mouthpiece. "No. Not now. But back then I guess I could. I don't know. It's all so vague. I just remember them telling me not to tell anyone, ever."

"What about your family? Do you remember them?"

"No…not really. Except…"

"Except?"

"I had an older brother. Marcus. Remember I said I liked your Marcus right away because of his name? That was why. It was my brother's name. I…I kept his picture."

Casey closed her eyes. It was almost enough… almost, but not quite.

"Your name isn't really Laura, is it, sweetie?"

"It is…now."

"And what was it before?"

"Sara," she whispered. "It was Sara…something. I—God, Casey, I can't talk about this anymore. Please…"

She heard the tears in her sister's voice. "Okay, honey. Okay, calm down. I'm sorry. I didn't mean to dredge all this up. I swear it." Laura sniffled. "Don't cry, sis."

"I'm not."

"Liar." Casey had to swipe at her own eyes. As she did, she glimpsed her watch. Her hour was up and then some. "You okay?"

"Yeah, fine. You're the one I'm worried about."

"I have a Guardian watching over me," Casey said.

"Well, I have a houseful of overprotective cowboys, so I guess we're both safe."

"I'll see you soon, little sister. Real soon. Promise."

"You'd better," Laura said.

Casey whispered goodbye and hung up the phone. Was it enough? Could this be true? Could her little sister possibly be the same Sara that Marcus was still mourning?

She should tell him.

No. She should get proof first.

I kept his picture.

Casey looked toward the ceiling as the realization hit her. The locket. The one Laura had always worn, until the day Casey had asked to see the picture inside. It had vanished after that. But she'd bet money her sister hadn't thrown it away.

She'd just go home, check the locket…

* * *

She walked through the front door, turned on the light, saw him and went cold inside. He sat on the sofa, staring straight ahead, his face a granite mask.

Then her gaze moved lower to the file folder open on the coffee table in front of him, the printouts spread around. Copies of news stories—every one she could find mentioning the Guardian. And the others—the ones about the murder of his family, the ones that gave his real name.

"I know what you're thinking, Marcus."

"Do you?"

She nodded. "But you're wrong. I can explain all of this."

He met her eyes, and his gaze was hard as steel. "You're going to say you aren't doing a story on me."

"I'm not. Check my computer files. I'll take you the office myself. There's no story."

He nodded, but she didn't think he believed her. "There is, however, a thorough investigation here."

She moved slowly, her knees wobbling. "Yes. I started trying to find out about you the day I met you." She tossed her purse on a nearby stand, but kept coming forward.

"But not for a story."

"No. Not for a story."

"Then why?"

She shoved the coffee table aside, knelt in front of him and cupped his hands. "You intrigued me. At first, it was my natural curiosity—I've never been able to stand a mystery."

"And what about the cruelty, Casey?"

She blinked in shock as he pulled his hands from beneath hers.

"You knew my last name. Knew it was Brand, and yet you took me out to that damned ranch anyway, just to gauge my reaction. Didn't you?"

She lowered her head. "I thought it was just a co-incidence at first. But...but it made me wonder. You told me you were missing a lot of your childhood memories. I thought if you saw the ranch, and if there was a connection, seeing the place might stimulate something."

"So it was for me. You subjected me to that for my sake."

She swallowed hard.

"And what about last night?"

She was confused. "We made love. And it was wonderful, Marcus, and—"

He turned his head sharply away from her. "Not that. Before, when you let me relive that—that night-mare. And all the time you already knew..."

"No. No, Marcus, I didn't know. I'd seen the newspaper account, yes, but I wasn't sure it was your family. And all of that is beside the point, anyway. Marcus, you *needed* to talk about it. You needed to..."

"No, I didn't." He still didn't look at her. Refused to face her.

Still kneeling, she cupped his face in her hands and turned him to her. "You're upset with me, aren't you?"

"You're damned right I am. And don't try to fix

everything with those big innocent, eyes, Casey, because I see right through them.''

"I'm glad. Because I see through yours, too. None of this would bother you so much if you didn't care about me just a little."

"Is this what happens when someone cares for you? You sneak around behind their back, pry into their private lives?"

"Search their houses while they go to the office?"

He snapped his eyes shut as if she'd struck him.

"I want to know everything there is to know about you, Marcus. I want to heal those wounds you keep working open. I want to give your past, your memories, back to you. I want to know you like no one else does." She threaded her fingers into his hair, stroking softly. "Can I help it if the only way I know how to deal with that sort of thing is by snooping? How can you hate me for it, Marcus, when you know it's because I've fallen in love with you?"

His eyes popped open, and he looked stricken.

"You do know that, don't you?"

Searching her face, he looked at her as if she were speaking a foreign language.

"If you'd just let yourself, I think you could love me, too."

"No. That's not going to happen. You can't just erase the past with a few words, Casey. That's not the way it works."

"Maybe not. But it doesn't change the way I feel. And don't be so sure I can't change the past. I'm pretty talented, you know."

He frowned, looking bewildered, under attack and

shell-shocked. She leaned forward and brushed his lips with hers. "If you want to, you can burn this stuff," she said, waving a hand at the folder. "It was never meant for anyone's eyes but mine, and I've seen it already."

He stared at her as if dumbfounded.

"Meanwhile, let me just go upstairs for a minute. I might have a Christmas present for you."

He tilted his head. She kissed him again, then got to her feet and walked away.

She could have been angry at him, probably would have been if she hadn't known so well what he was doing. Putting up barriers, looking for reasons not to love her. He was sinking fast and grasping at straws. And so wounded, in so much pain and incredibly afraid of being hurt even more.

She was going to make him so happy. She could hardly wait to see his face when she told him.

She didn't go to her own room but to her sister's. The jewelry box sat on the dresser. The answer was inside, probably had been all along.

She reached for the lid, opened it and dug through the contents in search of the locket. Her hands were trembling as she pried the tiny heart open to reveal the photograph inside. She sat down on the edge of the bed and stared at the photo, eyes watering.

There was a little boy and a little girl. The girl was unmistakably Laura, the boy a little older. He had dark hair and solemn dark brown eyes. His arm was around the little girl, and he looked like a younger version of Marcus.

Or was that wishful thinking?

Only one way to find out. Take it downstairs and show him.

She got to her feet.

The lights went out.

Damn her.

He couldn't even stay angry at her. Oh, sure, he could brood and bluster fine, right up until the second when she looked into his eyes or touched her lips to his. Explaining all his doubts away and making him want nothing more than to fall into her arms.

God, was she some kind of sorceress?

Or was she just so insightful that she saw things he didn't? She said he was wrong, that he could fall in love if he'd let himself. And damned if it didn't seem to Marcus as if that was exactly what was happening to him.

My God, could it be?

She loved him. He could hear her saying it again, so simply, so matter-of-factly, as if it were as natural as her smile or the sparkle in her eyes. Three simple words that had somehow plunged him into this ridiculous state of confusion and bewilderment.

Something had happened when she'd said those words to him. His heart had leaped in response. He was still afraid to love her. Still certain that self-preservation dictated he resist the temptation to love her. But he was beginning to wonder if that kind of thing was within his control. Maybe loving her wasn't a choice. Maybe he just…just did.

Imagine that.

The lights died, plunging him into familiar darkness. And he knew Mancini was near. His senses pricked to full alert, and he jumped to his feet. "Casey!"

And then Casey screamed, and his heart replayed the final scream of his mother. For just an instant, he was shut in the darkness of that basement, feet frozen to the floor, listening to the scream of a woman he loved. A woman who was the center of his universe.

But only for an instant.

"No," he whispered. "Not this time." And the next thing he knew, he was racing up the stairs, kicking in the bedroom door and standing there, breathless. In the moonlight streaming through the open bedroom window, he saw a brute of a man holding Casey from behind, a gun pressed to her temple.

"Let her go, Mancini."

The man's head came up fast. "How the hell do you know my name?"

"I heard my mother scream it just before you shot her dead, you son of a—"

"*Your* mother?"

"You took away everything I loved." He locked gazes with Casey. "But you won't do it again. Let her go, Mancini. If you hurt her, I'll make you wish to God you'd never been born."

"Sorry. She's a witness. But don't worry, you'll be joining her soon enough." He thumbed back the hammer.

"You've got the wrong woman, mister," Casey said, her voice strained. "My sister is far away from here, safe. Killing me isn't going to do you one bit of good."

"Wha—" He jerked Casey around quickly, searching her face in the moonlight.

She didn't waste a second. She brought her knee up hard and fast, right into his groin, and the second his grip on her eased, she dived to the right. Marcus launched himself forward. Mancini's finger clenched the trigger just as Marcus kicked the gun out of his hand. The gun went off, and he felt the breeze of the bullet blazing by his head. "Thank you, Caine. You were right all along," Marcus muttered.

Mancini reached for him, only to receive several rapid-fire blows to the face. The man's head snapped back, and he staggered backward.

Marcus saw what was about to happen, and in spite of himself, he reached for Mancini, but it was too late.

The man's bulk pulled him backward, and flailing his arms, Mancini smashed through the window. His wail filled the night, but only briefly. When his body thudded to the ground below, he went silent. Marcus stared at the motionless figure, his heart beating hard. He told himself it was over now, that he could let go of the past once and for all—and then he wondered why it didn't *feel* over at all.

Marcus turned, gripped Casey, pulled her gently into his arms. "Did he hurt you?"

"I'm okay…I'm okay now, Marcus. Just hold me."

He did, closing his arms more tightly around her, wishing he could hold her this way forever. "I was wrong before," he whispered, pushing back her hair and bending to kiss her forehead. "So wrong. I said I couldn't love you, but I do, dammit. You didn't give me any choice. I...I just couldn't see it until he had that gun to your head. God, when I thought of losing you..."

"Marcus." She stepped back, searching his face. "Do you mean it?"

He nodded, close to tears. It was as if he were alive again. "More than I can even believe."

"Thank God you told me now. If you'd waited, I'd have always wondered if it was real or...or just gratitude. And Laura..."

"Laura?"

She nodded hard, looking around the room and finally spotting something on the floor. She bent to pick it up, took his hand in hers and gently lowered the thing into his palm. A necklace, with a long silvery chain.

"You'll understand, I think. Once you see this."

He stared down at it, confused. "We have to call the police—an ambulance—"

"I'll do that. You get the lights back on and then take a look at the locket. Okay?"

He closed his hand around it. "I don't want to leave you alone for a minute." He took her hand in his free one and drew her downstairs. Pausing at the phone, he dialed in utter darkness, gave the address, told the 911 operator he needed police and an ambulance, then put the phone down before she could ask him to stay on the line.

He took Casey with him to the fuse box in the basement, where he tripped the breaker, and the lights came back on.

"Ready?" she asked him, reaching up to snap on the basement light.

"Sure." He wasn't sure what was in the locket. He didn't even care. He loved her, and he felt as if he were finally glimpsing a light at the end of his long, dark tunnel.

He lifted the locket, pried open the heart and then frowned down at a photo of himself and his sister, arm in arm. The pain flared anew, and he closed his eyes. Tears dampened his lashes anyway. "God...Oh God, Sara...." His lips thinning in undisguised agony, he let the tears spill over and reached up to stroke Casey's hair. "I don't know where you ever got this, but—"

"It's Laura's."

He tore his gaze from his sister's likeness and stared, puzzled, at Casey.

"Laura witnessed a murder when she was little. The police never let on that she hadn't been killed with the rest of her family. Instead they put her in the witness protection program, and she became my little sister. But before that...before all that, Marcus...her name was Sara."

His brows arched upward. "Sara?" It came out a croak.

She nodded. "Sara Brand. Somehow related to the Texas Brands, I think. And I think maybe they knew, and were instrumental in getting her placed with their old friends, the Joneses, who were close enough by so they could keep tabs on her."

"*My* Sara?"

"She was wearing this when she arrived, Marcus.

And I know that's her in the photo. I remember the way she looked—just like this, only sad, lost and so alone.''

He stared down at the photo and saw for the first time the woman in that little girl's face. Laura. His Sara. Then he searched Casey's eyes again. ''You don't have any idea what this means...''

''I figure after twenty-two years without a Christmas, you deserve a hell of a present this year. Besides, it's the least I can do for the man I love. Merry Christmas, Marcus.''

He pulled her into his arms and kissed her long and deep. He loved her. He did. And nothing would ever change it. God, what she'd given him. He could hold her, kiss her like this forever.

But she pulled away. ''Don't you think we'd better tell Laura—I mean, Sara—about this?''

He frowned. ''She doesn't know?''

''Not yet.'' She lowered her gaze.

''Hey.'' Marcus lifted her chin. ''You okay?''

''You love me. How can I not be okay?''

But he saw a slight shadow in her eyes beneath the joy and the love shining on him. And he thought maybe he knew what it was. He'd fix it, though. He'd fix everything for her from now on.

Epilogue

For the second time in a week, Marcus drove underneath the arches of the Texas Brand. Members of the family—his cousins—came streaming out onto the front porch. The place had Christmas lights glowing all over it, red and green, all of them turned on now that it was dark outside. A big old pine tree growing out front had been decked out and twinkled merrily. And for the first time in a long time, the Yuletide spirit touched him, tweaked his heart, made him smile.

He stopped the car and got out, Casey at his side, holding his hand, searching his face.

Laura ran forward into Casey's arms. "Thank God it's over," she whispered. "And you're okay."

"I wouldn't have been...if not for Marcus."

Laura smiled, turning toward Marcus, taking one of his hands. Hers felt warm. His mind flashed back...their hands, entwined. His skinny, hers still plump with baby fat.

"Thank you," she said.

"You'll have to tell us all about it...Marcus. Funny, you remind me a lot of a Marcus I used to know."

Marcus met Garrett Brand's eyes. "The one you taught to ride?"

Garrett's jaw dropped. He blinked. Casey took Garrett's arm and led him and the others aside, leaving Marcus alone, for the moment, with Laura. She was staring up at him, a puzzled frown across her brow.

He took the locket and placed it in her hands. "When your family was murdered, you were playing hide-and-seek. Your mother was looking for you, but I guess she didn't find you. I've been thinking on this, and I'll bet you crawled into the cupboard underneath the kitchen sink. She never could find you when you hid there."

Her eyes got a little wider. "H-how...?"

"Your brother was in the basement, so they didn't get him, either. But all this time, he thought you were dead. And you must have thought the same about him."

"M-my brother?" She looked stunned. "Marcus..."

"That's right."

"Marcus?" She searched his face and suddenly burst into tears and flung herself into his arms. Marcus held her close, rocking her, kissing her hair, so dark, just like his.

"It's okay, Sara. We're together now, and we'll never be apart again, I swear it."

She just kept saying his name, over and over again. And he held her until her tears subsided. It took a long time. Her sobs left her weak, and red-eyed, but smiling all over.

"You okay?" he asked when she finally settled down a bit.

She stared at him. "For the first time in a long time, I think I am."

"I know the feeling." Then, his arm around her, he turned and led her back to where the others stood staring in wonder. He guessed Casey had explained it all to them.

Garrett slapped his hat against his thigh. "Hot damn, Marcus, welcome back. Welcome home, cousin!"

Wes was slapping his shoulder next, and then Ben and Adam and Elliot, and even Jessi, though she had to be too young to remember him much.

He felt as if he really had come home, even though the Texas Brand had only been a place to visit as a child. He supposed it had always felt more like home than his parents' house in Silver City.

He stepped away, leaving them to fuss over his sister while he turned toward Casey.

She stood a little to the side, slightly away from the rest. He went to her, clasped her shoulders, searched her face.

"What is it, angel?"

She lowered her eyes. "I...don't belong here. I should go. This is a...a family thing."

"You are family."

"No—"

"Yes. You're my family, Casey. You just inherited a pile of long-lost cousins, is all."

She lowered her head. "It doesn't feel that way."

"No. Probably feels like you're losing your baby sister, huh?"

Sniffing, she nodded. "It's selfish, I know. And I really am happy for you and—"

He pulled her close and kissed her long and hard. And when he set her away, he looked deep into her eyes. "I guess I'll just have to make sure you don't ever feel that way again."

"How?"

Her eyes, so big, so *soft*, stared straight up into his.

"By marrying you. That way, this family thing… it'll be, you know, official."

She blinked as if in disbelief. "Marcus?"

"It took me twenty-two years to learn to love again. You gave my life back to me. If you think I'm going to let you get away, you'd better think again."

Her eyes fell closed, and she sank gently into his arms. "I can't believe this is true."

"Besides, I read in the personals that I was tired of a solitary existence and seeking a wife. And if it's in the paper, it has to be true. Right?"

She smiled up at him. "You think so?"

He nodded, swallowed hard, searched her face. "I'm serious here, Casey." Clasping her hand in his, he dropped to one knee. "I love you, Casey Jones. Will you be my wife?"

Her tears spilled over, and her smile wavered. "You know I will." She tugged him to his feet, and he pulled her into his arms and kissed her.

Around them, the Brands of Texas exploded in applause and whoops that could have been heard all the way back in Silver City.

"Looks like we have a new Brand in the family," Wes hollered.

"And a pair of old ones come back to the fold!" Ben added.

"I knew that feller looked familiar," Garrett mused.

Marcus turned, one arm around Casey, and draped the other one around Sara. "We have a Christmas to celebrate, ladies. And I, for one, plan to make it one to remember."

"It already is," Casey whispered. "It already is."

Graham sat near the hotel pool beneath an umbrella-shaded table with a drink in his hand. Beside him on the floor was a suitcase, and piled neatly in the next chair, two articles of clothing.

Marcus and Casey had phoned, but they hadn't told him anything he hadn't already guessed. They'd invited him to join them at the Brand ranch for the holiday celebrations, but Graham had other things to do.

Somewhere out there was another one.

A young boy, or perhaps even a girl, who'd lost everything, who had no one left. One in need of guidance. One receptive to the training. One who'd step into the Guardian's shoes one day.

Until then...

Graham eyed the wide-brimmed fedora and the long black coat. They'd worn well all these years. He only hoped they still fit.

*   *   *   *   *

Here's a preview of next month's

———World's Most———
Eligible Bachelors

Symon Cope
the brooding Montana playboy from

BIG SKY BILLIONAIRE
by
Jackie Merritt

Symon Cope parked his car and strode into the building through the glassed-in front doors. Inside he looked around. Several people were working behind a large circular counter, and he headed that way.

"Holy cow!" a young woman whispered to another. "Take a look at the hunk who just walked in."

"I'm in love," the other woman sighed with a mock swoon. "Who is he?"

"I have no idea, but I'm going to find out." She moved to a prominent place at the counter so Sy would have to talk to her.

Sy walked up without a smile. He was in no mood for chitchat of any kind, and he especially had no desire to flirt with this young woman, who looked as though that were her primary goal for the day. "Would you please contact Pamela Brooks and tell her that Symon Cope is in the lobby and would like to see her?"

The woman visibly gulped. "Symon Cope? Yes, Mr. Cope. I'll page her right away."

"Thank you."

Sy walked away and the woman rolled her eyes at her friend and mouthed, "Did you hear?" After receiving a silent nod, the first woman picked up the phone and punched two numbers. Sy could hear the page come through the public address system.

"Pamela Brooks, please come to the lobby. Mr. Symon Cope is...uh, he's waiting to see you."

The page echoing throughout the building made Pam's knees go weak. Not a single person in the entire center could have missed hearing it. Hurrying her step, she dashed into the appointed room and told her co-worker, "I have a page."

"I heard it. We'll talk later."

"Thanks." Leaving as hastily as she'd arrived, Pam made the first turn in the corridor before the reality of Sy's actually being there caught up with her. She ducked into an alcove to collect herself because she was shaking like a leaf and knew in her soul that she could not face Sy in a weak and sniveling state.

In fact, she had never needed emotional strength more than she did now. This wasn't her idea, she didn't like what was happening, and if Sy dared to imply anything else, she was going to let him have it.

Finally realizing that she could hide in this alcove all day and still not feel calm, Pam squared her shoulders, lifted her chin and reentered the corridor leading to the lobby. Her determination to maintain the upper hand in this confrontation stayed with her until she was at the immense entrance of the lobby and saw Sy, and then everything within her went to hell.

He wasn't looking her way; he was near one of the huge front windows staring outside. He was gorgeous, tall and straight and all man in dark blue jeans, a blue-and-white-striped shirt and low-heeled black boots.

His long hair was tied back with a leather string, and he was wearing sunglasses with black lenses.

There seemed to be a peculiar hush in the lobby, and Pam's eyes darted around to find out why. Everyone was watching her and Sy. People who shouldn't be in the lobby at all were peering around doors.

"Good Lord," she mumbled in abject disgust. Obviously everyone who'd heard the page and hadn't been involved in something that couldn't be left for a few minutes had come to the lobby to see the show.

Well, maybe she'd give them one, she thought angrily. Maybe she just might stand their hair on end.

The blustering resolve weakened the closer she got to Sy, however.

Hearing approaching footsteps, he turned from the window, fully prepared to treat Pam respectfully, but coolly until he knew what to do next.

But seeing her, looking into her beautiful green eyes and feeling her pull again completely destroyed his sensible intentions, and before he knew what he was doing, he had pulled her into his arms and kissed her fully on the lips.

Hearing a collective gasp from everyone in the lobby, Pam permitted the kiss to last only a few seconds. She didn't permit herself to enjoy it, although she would die on the spot before giving *that* away to her nosy co-workers.

The one thing she couldn't control was the burning heat in her cheeks. Glaring up at Sy, she whispered furiously, "You still believe you can do anything you want! Let go of me, you cretin!"

It finally sank into Sy's brain that a dozen people

were watching them. He'd embarrassed Pam in front of the people with whom she worked, and he was embarrassing himself.

But even red-faced, he felt a crazy kind of joy. Any woman trying to trap a man into marrying her would not be calling him names!

"Pam," he said in an undertone. "I have a very important question to ask you."

Fill your holiday with...
excitement, magic and love!

Mistletoe Kisses

December is the time for Christmas carols, surprises
wrapped in colored paper and kisses under the mistletoe.
Mistletoe Kisses is a festive collection of stories about three
humbug bachelors and the feisty heroines who entice them
to ring in the holiday season with love and kisses.

AN OFFICER AND A GENTLEMAN
by Rachel Lee

THE MAGIC OF CHRISTMAS
by Andrea Edwards

THE PENDRAGON VIRUS
by Cait London

Available December 1998
wherever Harlequin and Silhouette books are sold.

Take 2 bestselling love stories FREE

Plus get a FREE surprise gift!

Special Limited-Time Offer

Mail to Silhouette Reader Service™

3010 Walden Avenue
P.O. Box 1867
Buffalo, N.Y. 14240-1867

YES! Please send me 2 free Silhouette Romance™ novels and my free surprise gift. Then send me 6 brand-new novels every month, which I will receive months before they appear in bookstores. Bill me at the low price of $2.90 each plus 25¢ delivery and applicable sales tax, if any.* That's the complete price, and a saving of over 10% off the cover prices—quite a bargain! I understand that accepting the books and gift places me under no obligation ever to buy any books. I can always return a shipment and cancel at any time. Even if I never buy another book from Silhouette, the 2 free books and the surprise gift are mine to keep forever.

215 SEN CH7S

Name	(PLEASE PRINT)	
Address	Apt. No.	
City	State	Zip

This offer is limited to one order per household and not valid to present Silhouette Romance™ subscribers. *Terms and prices are subject to change without notice. Sales tax applicable in N.Y.

USROM-98

©1990 Harlequin Enterprises Limited

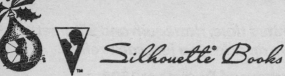

For a limited time, Harlequin and Silhouette have an offer you just can't refuse.

In November and December 1998:

BUY **ANY** TWO HARLEQUIN
OR SILHOUETTE BOOKS and
SAVE $10.00
off future purchases

OR BUY ANY THREE HARLEQUIN OR SILHOUETTE BOOKS
AND **SAVE $20.00** OFF FUTURE PURCHASES!

(each coupon is good for $1.00 off the purchase of two
Harlequin or Silhouette books)

JUST BUY 2 HARLEQUIN OR SILHOUETTE BOOKS, SEND US YOUR
NAME, ADDRESS AND 2 PROOFS OF PURCHASE (CASH REGISTER
RECEIPTS) AND HARLEQUIN WILL SEND YOU A COUPON BOOKLET
WORTH $10.00 OFF FUTURE PURCHASES OF HARLEQUIN OR
SILHOUETTE BOOKS IN 1999. SEND US 3 PROOFS OF PURCHASE AND
WE WILL SEND YOU 2 COUPON BOOKLETS WITH A TOTAL SAVING OF
$20.00. (ALLOW 4-6 WEEKS DELIVERY) OFFER EXPIRES
DECEMBER 31, 1998.

I accept your offer! Please send me a coupon booklet(s), to:

NAME: _____

ADDRESS: _____

CITY: _____ STATE/PROV.: _____ POSTAL/ZIP CODE: _____

Send your name and address, along with your cash register
receipts for proofs of purchase, to:

In the U.S.	In Canada
Harlequin Books	Harlequin Books
P.O. Box 9057	P.O. Box 622
Buffalo, NY	Fort Erie, Ontario
14269	L2A 5X3

PHQ4982

MEN at WORK

All work and no play?
Not these men!

October 1998
SOUND OF SUMMER by Annette Broadrick

Secret agent Adam Conroy's seductive gaze
could hypnotize a woman's heart. But it was
Selena Stanford's body that needed saving—
when she stumbled into the middle of an
espionage ring and forced Adam out of
hiding....

November 1998
GLASS HOUSES by Anne Stuart

Billionaire Michael Dubrovnik never lost a
negotiation—until Laura de Kelsey Winston
changed the boardroom rules. He might
acquire her business...but a kiss would cost
him his heart....

December 1998
FIT TO BE TIED by Joan Johnston

Matthew Benson had a way with words
and women—but he refused to be tied
down. Could Jennifer Smith get him to
retract his scathing review of her art by
trying another tactic: tying him *up?*

Available at your favorite retail outlet!

MEN AT WORK™

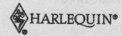 

Look us up on-line at: http://www.romance.net   PMAW3

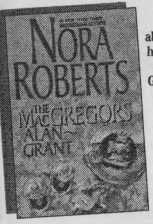

Bestselling author

LINDSAY McKENNA

continues the drama and adventure of her popular series with an all-new, longer-length single-title romance:

MORGAN'S MERCENARIES

HEART OF THE JAGUAR

Major Mike Houston and Dr. Ann Parsons were in the heat of the jungle, deep in enemy territory. She knew Mike's warrior blood kept him from the life—and the love—he silently craved. And now she had so much more at stake. For the beautiful doctor carried a child. His child...

Available in January 1999, at your favorite retail outlet!

Look for more MORGAN'S MERCENARIES in 1999, as the excitement continues in the Special Edition line!

™ *Silhouette*®

PSMORGMERC